Accidents of Time and Place

By
S. Paul Klein

PUBLISH
AMERICA

PublishAmerica
Baltimore

ISBN: 1-4241-7745-6
PUBLISHED BY PUBLISHAMERICA, LLLP
www.publishamerica.com
Baltimore

Printed in the United States of America

Dedication

For Diane, who has always known it was just a matter of time.

Acknowledgment

The author especially acknowledges the help and support of the Highland Writer's Group, where Hector first found his voice.

Chapter 1 - New Rhondda

When the wind blows in New Rhondda, it carries the grit and acidic breath of the mines. There is a darkness in the air and on the ground that isn't noticed until it is there, ingrained in the surface. It is seen by those who go there, but not by those who are born to it. The chill of fall and the heart of winter can mix to form a grey, etching mist that settles on lives as well as on things.

The red and cream Trailways bus pulled into the parking space and eased to a stop at the back of the bus station, on the hill overlooking the town. It was dark, a frosty October night in the mine-pierced mountains, and the steaming windows of the all-night restaurant beckoned, but not to Hector Collin. Taking his small suitcase from the luggage compartment under the bus, he stepped out into the sparkling darkness.

The long street that began on Terminal Hill crossed the railroad tracks that bisected the town, and climbed the other side. New Rhondda sat in a bowl, the mines tunneled under the streets, and the tipples and elevator houses stood silhouetted against the sky in every direction.

Three blocks above the center of town the young man turned north onto a narrow, poorly paved street of small frame houses. Old trees kept the yards in shade, even on a bright full-moon night like this. Dogs barked once or twice, sensing a stranger passing by, but none challenged him. At his parents' house he turned, walked up the slate path from the street, and knocked on the door.

After the surprise of his appearance at the front door for the first time in almost 20 years, Hector was accepted without question or demand. He simply was back. It had taken his mother only a few minutes to move things around in his old room before he was reestablished in it. Hector offered no explanation, and his parents sought none. He soon fell into the first uninterrupted sleep he had known in weeks and did not awaken until his father called him for supper in the early evening of the next day.

Wearing the same clothes he had traveled in, Hector joined his parents at the table. As the food was passed, his father, before starting to eat, said simply, "If you plan to stay, I've a place on the shift for you. You can start tonight."

Hector looked up from his plate, and said, "No. I'll not be in the mine. I'm just here for a little while." His father nodded, returned to his food, and said nothing more.

The older man ate quickly and silently. When he had finished, he put down his fork, stared thoughtfully at his son, and said: "Time you had a real job, isn't it son?"

"Sir?"

"We all know about that book you wrote, but what else did college do for you? What else can you do?"

"I don't know, Daddy. I don't really know."

"Then you'd better come with me tonight, son."

"No."

His father looked at him with some surprise. This boy—this man now—had never said "no" to his father; had never offered a different opinion. But of course his son was now older, had been away from home, in the army. Experience had changed him.

Leaving the table without further conversation, the man did the things he did every night before leaving for work. Then he stepped out into the night, his lunch pail in his hand, his helmet on his head, and closed the door.

The next morning Hector was up at first light. In the kitchen he heard his father and mother exchange a few words, and he knew that the older man had returned from his shift and was on his way to bed. Dressing in old pants, his old sweater and brown shoes, Hector came downstairs. The two men nodded as they met on the stair, and Hector walked into the kitchen.

At the worn kitchen table, where Hector had eaten every breakfast of his life until he was almost 18, he found a plate and coffee cup waiting for him where they had always been. He looked around the kitchen, expecting to see some change, but he found instead, only his mother and himself. The man had come home to find the boy, but the boy wasn't there, only the man.

"Your—" She paused, finding the word unfamiliar to her. "Your wife not coming here?"

"Not now, Mama." "Mama" sounded unfamiliar to her, too. "She's working."

"Will you stay long?"

"I don't know. I'm just looking around." If his mother found that obscure, she said nothing. It wasn't part of her world to have a man's full confidence perhaps, or maybe it was just that she knew, as she had discovered with her husband, that in time she would learn what she needed to know, and that satisfied her for now.

Chapter 2 - Washington, DC

L ook out over the 69 square miles that make up Washington, D.C. A few low hills surround a bowl that empties into the Potomac River. It can be a damp and cold place in the winter, a damp and hot place in the summer. By 1955, more than a century-and-a-half after it was first laid out, it was still at heart a small Southern town. There were museums and art galleries, and even a theater or two, and the words that floated in the air came from every corner of the earth, but it was still small, and still just a town.

The commercial buildings along K Street in Northwest Washington were mostly converted townhouses, many with a few apartments or professional offices in the upper stories. The Vienna had been built as a restaurant and so was entered at street level, rather than up a half flight of stairs as most of the old houses were built. That set it apart and gave it a more legitimate, businesslike appearance. It was narrow and deep, having replaced a townhouse by occupying the same footprint even though the bricks and plaster were new. Booths lined both sides of the long room, with square tables for four in the middle. At the back was the dividing wall separating the kitchen from the dining room. A glass-fronted counter extended from the entrance parallel to the side wall, making a small, enclosed space for the cash register. Behind the glass in neat rows were five brands of chewing gum, an open box with rolls of mints, opened boxes of candy bars and finally, neatly arrayed packets of aspirin and anti-acid. A divider split the display case, and on the other side were cigars and cigarettes, formally set out in their boxes and half-cartons. On top of the counter was a small vase with a fresh flower, taller than the display rack holding book matches with the restaurant name on the cover, and a chrome-plated toothpick dispenser that stood beside it.

Hector Collin sat at his usual table toward the middle, on one side of the poorly lit restaurant, facing the mirrored wall. On the table beside him was a note pad and a gold-capped fountain pen. When not using it, he placed the pen neatly beside the pad, and if he wasn't ready to eat, looked around, using the mirror to see what was going on in the room. He seldom made eye contact with anyone, and if he did, he simply blinked, and then moved his gaze elsewhere. Often he would return to his pad and make a quick note, a word or two, or a short half sentence.

It was that quiet part of the day, the time before a restaurant fills each evening, when the early regulars begin drifting in. Mostly the Vienna served the people who lived in the neighborhood, or who worked near Washington Circle. Many of the regulars, like Hector, had started coming as students when they were at the university. For Hector, it was also convenient to his room across the street in one of the old residential hotels. Behind him, the waitress gathered a glass of water and her order pad, a menu and her pencil and approached the table. Without preamble she announced: "Meatloaf tonight. It's Monday. That okay?" Jane was the kind of girl (she was still in her twenties) who long ago had found the work that satisfied her. Here in the Vienna she felt comfortable around the regulars, knowing when to suggest something other than the special, or to let someone like Hector sit for a quarter of an hour before taking his order. At her question, the man simply nodded, looking up briefly in the mirror. No smile, no flicker of recognition just a nod, then back to his small note pad. Whatever curiosity the girl had, she learned early on not to try getting beyond the level of intimacy her customers permitted. She said, "Thanks," and as she walked to the kitchen, pulled off the order to hand through the window. It hadn't been necessary to write more than the table number and "special" across the page.

His food before him, Hector put his pen down and concentrated on the meal. He ate silently, stolidly, not hurrying, exactly, but not pausing more than necessary to chew and swallow. Occasionally he would stop and take a sip from the coffee cup beside the plate, but generally he ate without stopping. There was no sense of urgency in his eating, nor a mechanical action, though he did eat in a peculiar pattern perhaps: first the green vegetable, then the starch, then the meat. His way of eating was a reflection of the man's whole approach to life; fixed, methodical, an unconscious act of renewal three times a day.

Valery owned the restaurant with her husband. Most of the day she stood at her post, greeting the customers with a word and a smile. Regulars like Hector sat at tables they thought of as "theirs." So regular were these people that if they didn't come in, Valery held the table for at least half-an-hour before seating someone else there. Once in a while a stranger would ask for a particular table, but if it was one of the regulars the hostess would say that it was "reserved." Even though a regular might take a table for four during a busy period, she would never think of hurrying him, or asking if he would mind if she seated a stranger there. The regulars, after all, were the heart of the Vienna.

His solitary meal finished, Hector sat for perhaps another quarter of an hour before gathering his pad and pen, leaving a small tip, and going to the counter to pay his bill. Always the hostess would ask, "Everything okay?" To which Hector would simply nod, and murmur what sounded like "umpf." Taking his change, he then walked out the door and into the evening. Valery would follow him with her eyes until he moved beyond the field of vision framed by the restaurant doorway. Regardless of the weather, Hector would walk away from the restaurant, down the block to the corner. From there he crossed over to the other side, then turning back in the direction of the restaurant, he would walk back up the long block to the gray stone building where he lived.

Chapter 3 - The King of Rumania

It was spring, and along K Street the south-facing windows were open to let the warm breezes in. The air at this time of year was always full of the freshness of a new season. Even in the city there was a mix of turned earth, newly cut grass, and the perfume of early-flowering plants.

At his window overlooking the street, Hector sat at his desk in his room at the King of Rumania Hotel. Although the desk faced the window, he seldom looked beyond the curtains, and except on the hottest of summer days, the sash remained closed. Not cold by nature, nor warm, Hector was simply unaware of his personal comfort. Most days he wore the same brown sweater, corduroy trousers and an open-necked shirt. When he did become uncomfortable, which was seldom, he would remove the sweater or add a coat. The coat was the army field jacket he had kept when he left the service. It was worn, comfortable, and faded except where his sergeant's stripes and division patches had kept the olive drab color fresh.

Hector attended classes most nights at the university's downtown campus four blocks up K Street and over two. Otherwise, his world was reasonably close and circumscribed: across the street to eat, up a few doors to a small office supply store where he would buy paper and notebooks, or to a drug store a block away; these were the limits of most of his daily life.

Occasionally he would venture further downtown to the public library some 17 or 18 blocks away, or to one of the movie theaters east of the White House. Rarely did his work or his interest take him beyond those places. When it did he usually walked. There were still streetcars on the rails of the city, and a reasonably direct bus route he could take to classes at the university's main campus near the northwest edge of the District, but Hector was by choice a pedestrian, preferring the solitude of the sidewalk to even a modest introduction of the social contract that public transportation would put into his daily life.

On the small rectangular desk, Hector had arranged this part of his life, as well. The centerpiece was an old Royal portable typewriter. The frame was highly polished black enamel, with gold leaf curlicues and lines decorating it. The keys were round, with black letters on a white background behind a celluloid lens, each with a chrome ring to hold the combination together. Behind and to the left of the machine sat a box of typing paper. There was also a box of carbon paper, and another box of thin, yellow paper. These were stacked in a wire rack on which Hector had splurged in a desire for neatness and order. On the far right corner of the desk was another box. In it were typed pages, to which he now added another, separating the carbon and second sheet before laying the white paper in the box. The yellow onionskin copy went into a drawer on the right side of the desk. Except for his uniform of the day, this could have been any company sergeant's desk, in any headquarters in the army. It was what went on the paper that was different.

15

Assembling a clean white sheet, a carbon and a yellow sheet, Hector fed them into the typewriter, rolling the platen using the carriage return. The feel of the movement, and the "chunk" sound the gears made pleased him. Perhaps it was evidence that he was accomplishing something. With the fresh sheet of paper before him in the typewriter, Hector picked up the finished pages. He began each session by reading what he had last written, so that he could resume the rhythm and direction of the chapter:

Chapter 7 (he wrote at the top of the page) -

A STRANGE BREED OF CATS

The Crystal is typical of the places older students gather. Instead of fraternity houses, full of teenagers bent on proving their capacity for beer, these men (and women, too) had done that in enlisted, NCO, and Officers Clubs when they were that age. "Grown-up" bars and restaurants, located away from the college campus, now replaced the military clubs. Here, however, there were no barriers based on rank or station. The criteria was compatibility.

Just off Dupont Circle and Connecticut Avenue, the Crystal was a common meeting ground for students from the universities with down-town campuses. A single rectangular room, presided over by the owner, a Greek named George, the restaurant was a mix of booths and square tables. There was no back room, no stage. The Crystal served simple, basic food. George presided over the bar, but these were mostly beer drinkers. Few could afford a steady diet of whiskey or cocktails. There were always a few students having lunch or dinner, but most of the regulars came in later, after evening classes were over. There was an international cast to the clientele. Many of the students were studying history, political science, or international relations. The mix of nationalities gave the restaurant a slightly exotic feel.

On this particular day, at about two in the afternoon, Don, a psychology major, was killing an hour before his afternoon class at the downtown campus. At 35, he didn't look like a college student. His face was that of an office worker, pale and a little puffy, thin blonde hair combed straight back from a high forehead. A coffee cup, half filled, sat before him, as did the textbook for his class. It was a basic statistics class, which he was finding useful at his part-time job in a local brokerage firm. Immersed in its pages, he hardly acknowledged the person who was sitting opposite him.

JoAnn's dark complexion, black hair and high cheek bones proclaimed her membership in one of the tribes of the Southwest. As Don studied his text, JoAnn studied him. Their relationship had been on and off for the last three years. Especially when Don was "out of bread" (he spoke in the patois of the jazz trumpeter he was on weekends), he would move in with JoAnn and her young daughter, Rose. His worldly belongings fit easily into an old "B-4" bag and his trumpet case. Rooms by the week, at places like the Cairo, suited his nature very well. Today the woman was waiting for him to finish studying so that they could talk.

A hubbub of voices at the cash register caused Don to look up. A police officer was showing George a piece of paper and asking him questions. Don looked back at his book, but said in a very low voice, "I think the law is looking for somebody. Just be cool. Ice the man." JoAnn, never an easy person to read, continued to sit impassively, looking at nothing.

The officer approached the table. He knew these two. Occasionally JoAnn's reserve crumbled, often after a night of drinking. Usually it was a neighbor who called the precinct house. JoAnn, with or without Don, lived in an apartment above a restaurant located three or four blocks north on the avenue.

Some of the puffiness in the man's face stemmed from JoAnn's Friday night fights.

"Hello Don. Hello Princess. Nice to see you two getting along." JoAnn, perhaps legitimately a princess in her tribe, continued to stare ahead. Don turned an impassive face to the cop and said nothing. "Looking for one of your drinking buddies," he said. "Xavier Belinky. Know where he is?"

Don looked up from his book again. "Like, what was that name man?"

"Belinky. Xavier."

"Ex-ay-vee-or." Don repeated the name, emphasizing each syllable precisely the same. "Never heard of him, man."

"Short guy, curly hair. Comes in here a lot with a girl named Tiger."

"Man, do you mean 'Ex'? Never knew him as 'Xavier' man."

"Yeah, that's him."

"Haven't seen him in a week, man," Don went on. "What's the cat done that Mr. Law wants him?"

"A and B. Simple assault and battery. Evidently he and this Tiger got into it pretty heavy last night and she's over at the hospital. Swore out a warrant for Ex-ay-vee-or," the officer said, mimicking Don's studied pronunciation. "If you know where I can find him, put me on the track. I'd like to serve this," waving the folded paper, "before I go off duty at seven." "Yeah, man. We'll let you know if we eyeball him. But I got to go to class." Don stood up, closed his book and smiled at JoAnn. "See you later. And if I see that bad cat, I'll send him your way," he said to the officer.

At the corner, Don fished in his pocket for a nickel and stepped into the phone booth that stood there. Three nickels later he had managed to reach two of the others in his small circle who knew Ex, and warned them their friend needed to get out of town.

It felt, to Don, like a scene from a spy movie. He met Bertrand and Ex behind a pillar in the back of Union Station. Ex had decided to go to New Jersey for a while to stay with his sister. Bertrand had reputedly been a member of the French Maquis (the underground network of partisans and political factions that had fought the Nazis in Occupied France). Such "escapes" were not new for him. He had purchased the ticket, Don had picked Ex up in an alley near the man's apartment, and at the last minute, before the "fugitive" walked to the train, they had traded jackets. Safely on his way, Don and Bertrand headed back to the Crystal.

For the next three hours, Hector continued working, the words rolling out, filling the pages. The typing skills Hector had learned as an army clerk gave him a facility with the machine. He could think the words without having to focus on getting the letters down and in the right place. Each day the manuscript grew, and now numbered more than 100 pages.

The story was populated by the people Hector had come to know during his university years. Now a senior, he was, like many he wrote about, facing the adult world. He had not come to college to become a writer. The "work in progress" had begun as an exercise for an English class in his junior year. A few sketches of his fellow students, especially those who were on the GI Bill, and thus a little older, had grown into what now looked to be a major work. Encouraged by his professor, Hector found more and more fulfillment in the work. Writing suited this quiet, solitary man. He wrote of his generation, the men and women who came of age in the 40's, because it was what he knew, but also because it was his way of trying to understand who they were, and what they were supposed to do, now that they were going to be "in charge."

They had been born before or at the beginning of the Depression, and they had grown to adolescence or even adulthood between 1942 and 1953; between the time World War II had begun and the war in Korea had ended. They hadn't known how to describe themselves when they returned from the wars. Hector did that for them.

He told of their abrupt rebirth as new people, forged in service as fighters and those who made the fighting possible. Even on the homefront, even in the civilian world, the children who became adults as war workers, as factory hands—women especially—found themselves recast, not as the people they had been taught to emulate—their mothers and fathers—but independent, and of a new world. A world their younger siblings could not always understand.

They were newly born, newly created, as grownups, with a past and a future and a large block of their lives that had been put on hold while they went to war. It was of those Hector had written, and it was for them that the book had the greatest meaning. In the end other books would be better known, other authors more honored, because they wrote about their war. Hector wrote about their peace.

Without meaning to, without wanting to, he would become a hero to these people. It was a fundamental part of his character, to take on without considering the consequences, a job from which others might run. It was simply another unplanned event in his life. Just as had been his decision to settle in the nation's capital.

Chapter 4 - In the Lobby

The King of Rumania had not been a transient hotel for many years, but the dark oak registration desk, and the framed opening that rose above it, still looked as it had when travelers were the hotel's main business. The plastered walls around the desk and window were once a creamy white, but now only seemed bright in contrast to the dark wood. Standing behind the desk, one could see the double glass doors to the left that led to the street. Across from that was the broad staircase, with its worn carpeting and dark wood bannister. The wood had felt the caress of so many hands that it no longer showed its grain, but was simply dark, almost black. In Washington's humid weather the wood became sticky if a hand rested on it too long. To the right of the desk was another set of double doors, leading to the first floor rooms. Behind the desk a door next to the wall of pigeonholes led to a small office, the manager's private domain, a place she seldom entered during the day.

A small area to the right of the front doors and to the left of the staircase held four overstuffed sofas, set in a square around a low table. Two armchairs on either side of a small round table were placed at the hotel's street-facing front window. Against the wall that formed the third side of the small lobby was an ornate mantel, surrounding a bricked-over fireplace; a relic of the hotel's early days. What light there was came from the window, the glass doors, and a black iron chandelier suspended from the ceiling in the middle of the lobby area. Except on sunny days, the lobby was less than inviting as a place to sit, especially if one wanted to read the daily paper put on the low table each morning. But the King of Rumania was clean, the beds reasonably comfortable, and the atmosphere anonymous, or at least it seemed that way.

Mary McAllister was a brassy woman, a little on the heavy side, more made-up than the time of day called for. Her earrings were large gold gypsy hoops, emphasized by her upswept and coiled blonde (too blonde) hair. The fleshy face seemed even rounder, sitting out so nakedly on her neck. Mary finished sorting the mail, putting envelopes into the pigeon holes that covered the wall behind the front desk. Now she turned and looked out into the lobby. Handing over the mail was a daily ritual. For Mary it was an excuse for prying into the lives of her "guests."

Hector was just coming down the stairs as Mary was putting the last letter in its pigeon hole. Turning, she called out to him, "Oh, Mr. Collin, there's a letter for you." In her hand she held a simple white envelope of notepaper size. Not a business letter, she knew. "It looks to be from Pennsylvania. Isn't that where you're from? I hope everything is well at home," she added as she handed him the letter. To her dissatisfaction, he took the letter and the other mail and returned up the stairs. Putting the rest of the mail on his desk, Hector put the unopened letter in his pocket, and returned to the lobby. Without a word to the manager, who watched from her position behind the registration desk, he turned at the bottom of the stairs and walked out through the double doors to the street.

It was nearing lunch time, and so Hector retraced his steps of the night before, down K Street to the corner, across and back up to the Vienna. Today, instead of putting out his note pad and pen, he retrieved the small envelope, opened it and began to read.

Dear Brother, it read, *I have wonderful news, and I hope you will agree. I have been offered a job (finally) in the Department of Defense, in Washington! I'm going to be an intelligence analyst, so that college education your monthly allotment paid for will finally be put to good use.* Hector tried to visualize his young sister, now about 24, he thought. But he hadn't been home since he had joined the army more than fourteen years ago. He recalled a slender - no, a thin - young girl, dark-haired like the pictures he remembered of his mother when she was young. *I will be coming to the city on Tuesday,* the letter went on, *and I will start work on the following Monday. I have to be "processed" first, though. I don't know if you have room, but could I stay with you until I find a room somewhere? Mama and Daddy are still against my leaving, but I think it will be okay with them if they know you are looking after me. You won't really have to, of course, but they think I still need to be "protected," whatever that means!! Anyway, I will be coming in by Greyhound at 5:30 in the afternoon.*

Pulling out a pocket calendar, Hector realized that this was Tuesday, then checked his wrist watch. It was just about half past eleven. He wondered for a moment where the letter had been. Looking at the envelope, he saw that it had only the street address, not the hotel name. Washington, being divided into four quadrants, has many streets with the same name that could be found in Northwest and Northeast, or Southwest and Southeast. But the letter had found him in time, anyway.

Hector put down the letter and stared into the mirror. This time, instead of surveying the other diners, he looked at nothing. It must have been evident from his expression, because Jane, seeing the open letter, came closer and said, "Not bad news I hope?" Her words, so similar to Mary McAllister's only half an hour ago, conveyed concern rather than curiosity. Hector blinked and turned slightly to look at the girl in the mirror. He smiled briefly, and shook his head.

"No," he said, "just a letter from my sister, and a slight problem." His voice, Jane noted, was not commanding or strong or even very loud, but was pleasant sounding. It was the first time she had really heard him say more than two or three words at a time. "She's coming to town and expects to stay with me."

"And that's a problem?"

Hector considered the question. "Well, I live across the street at the King of Rumania, and I just have a small bedroom. And I know there are no empty rooms right now, either."

Prompted perhaps by her generosity, or even her curiosity about Hector, Jane surprised herself when she offered: "I have a large apartment in an old house over in Southwest. She could stay with me for a few days, if that would help."

Chapter 5 - Reunion

If there was an American dream, it was blasted and dug out of the hills in the anthracite counties north and west of Philadelphia, up the Schulykill River. Bohemians, Russians, Poles, Irish and Welch, Italians and Germans found their way there. Some came individually, others in what amounted to whole villages. New Rhondda was one of those.

The dream was what connected them to their history, to their past, to their families "back home." It was why the parents or grandparents had come to America in the first place. And no matter what a child did on graduating from high school (and nearly all of them did), the first one out would be responsible for helping the next one. If the oldest was a boy, he would probably go down into the mines, but his weekly paycheck would come up to the family.

In the same way, when Hector left to join the army, a major part of his monthly pay went into an allotment sent regularly to his family. And in the Collin family, as in so many others of that valley, the money was not to put food on the table, or to buy frivolous things. It was hoarded and saved until the next child was ready to leave high school and go to college. It might be secretarial school or business college, but it was, in many families, the first step on the way to becoming a doctor or lawyer or college professor. For these people had a great belief in making the future better than the past. They wanted more for their children than they had had. They wanted it not in material things, but in stature and status. To be able to live above ground, was how it was often put. To live in the light.

Sis Collin sat by the big window, opened enough to feel the breeze that brought the last scent of coal dust into the bus. Leaning back against the firm seat, she let the freshening air help her make the transition from the hills to the city. It was not her first trip away from home. That had been six years earlier, when she left to go to college.

Sis had used Hector's allotment to go to the state university. She had graduated and returned home to teach history to 9th and 10th graders, but it was not what she wanted. She applied for a government job, and her degree in history brought an offer of a position as an intelligence analyst in one of the military departments. It wasn't what she had set out to do, but it was where she would go to fulfill her parents' dream. A dream that was hers, as well. Family? Children? They could wait. Would she give it all up for that? First came the desire to be someone, somewhere beyond the mines. Then the rest could come later.

The hands on the clock over the doors leading to the buses read 6:45 when Sis walked into the terminal. She carried a small suitcase made of hardened, varnished paper. It was brown in stripes of various widths and shades. The girl walked with an obvious stiffness shared by most people who have spent long hours on buses in interstate travel, but every step relieved a little more of the effects of her trip.

Standing in the center of the terminal, where he could watch all the doors, Hector presented himself as if on parade: stiffly, with his feet together, arms by his sides, thumbs along the seams of his none-too-pressed corduroys. Sis had no trouble recognizing him, though it was obvious from his expression that it was taking him some time to adjust his remembered image of his sister to match the tall, pretty girl who was walking toward him, smiling. It was the smile that he identified first. By then she was in front of him.

"Hello, Hector," she said.

"Hello, Sis." His reply was matter-of-fact, as if he had just seen her an hour ago. "Trip okay?"

"Yes."

"Fine."

Then, dropping her suitcase, Sis threw her arms around her brother and gave him a hug. "Oh, Hector, I'm so glad to be here, and so excited!" She pulled away, a little disconcerted by the stiffness of Hector's body in response to her greeting. "Is it okay that I'm here?" she asked uncertainly.

"Uh, oh yeah. Sure. I...I...it's been a long time, Sis." He looked down at the young girl before him. "I just got your letter in this morning's mail. I just wasn't expecting to see you I guess, after so long." Then he reached for her suitcase, picked it up and turned toward the street. "Do you have another suitcase?"

"No, I thought I'd wait until I got settled, then Mama can send me whatever else I have. It isn't much, though, anyway. Not much to dress for in New Rhondda."

Leaving the terminal building, they stepped out onto the sidewalk. An empty cab pulled up from the rank, and Hector, quickly weighing the cost of the ride against the long trip by bus or streetcar, opened the door and motioned Sis inside. Getting in with the small suitcase between them, he said, "The Vienna, on K Street, please. You know it?"

"Yessah," the cabby answered in his soft Southern accent.

As the Plymouth pulled away from the curb, Sis looked out the window, then said, "I thought you lived in a place called The King of Rumania."

"I do," he replied, settling back in the seat. "The Vienna is a restaurant where I eat. The King of Rumania is a hotel nearby." Sis continued to look at the big buildings crowding the streets as the taxi worked its way west in the late rush hour traffic.

"I'd kind of like to freshen up a bit before we go out to eat, if that's okay?" she said. "Can't we go to the hotel first? Besides, I have my suitcase, too."

The cab swung around the White House, then turned briefly north before turning left onto K Street. Hector looked out the window on his side, and then said, "Look, Sis, I don't want you to think you're unwelcome, but I just got your letter today, and frankly, I haven't thought about having you stay with me. I live in one room, by myself. But I have a—" Hector hesitated, "a friend who works at the Vienna, and she's offered to put you up for a few days 'til you get settled. But she doesn't get off work until ten o'clock." He turned his attention to the view through the windshield. Sis self-consciously smoothed her hair with her right hand as she turned to look at her brother.

"Mama and Daddy said I could come because you would look out for me."

Hector pulled out his wallet and counted out a dollar and some coins, the fare for the single zone ride. "I am looking out for you," he said. "This girl is very nice and she has a large apartment. It'll be fine." The cab turned across the roadway and pulled up in front of the Vienna.

Chapter 6 - Jane's Apartment

The building sat right on the sidewalk, as did most of the others on the block. It had once been an imposing place, only a few long blocks from the capitol building. Now, after perhaps half a century of use, both the neighborhood and the house looked worn and a little out of date. The white wooden siding hadn't aged well; Washington's climate is not kind to either buildings or people. But this was a spring night. The two rivers that joined a few blocks to the south, the ornamental trees that blossomed by late March, and the low silhouette of the skyline at night always provided a kind of magical atmosphere in the spring.

"It's so nice of you to let me stay with you," Sis was saying. They were walking up the steps from the street to the front door. Jane unlocked the big door and it swung inward. In the dim light of a ceiling fixture Sis could see the narrow stairs that began in the hall. On either side were wide sliding doors, now closed, that opened into the front rooms. Jane led the way up the stairs to the second floor, and turned to the right. Even in the poor light, it was obvious that this had once been a large home with many rooms.

"My apartment is this side of the hall," Jane said, indicating the three doors that faced them.

"It's big," Sis offered.

Jane had unlocked the middle door and turned on the light, revealing a square room with doors at either side, leading to the rest of the apartment. There were no windows in this room, which served as a living room, but Sis could see, through the open doors, light coming from the street in the front room, and from windows in the far wall of the room at the back. Compared with the Collin home in New Rhondda, in fact, the rooms seemed enormous.

"The bathroom and a small kitchen are through there," Jane said, indicating the door leading to the back of the house. I sleep in here," she said, showing Sis into the room overlooking the street. "If you don't mind sharing the room, I think you'll be comfortable." The large room with its nearly floor to ceiling windows held two single beds, the one nearest the windows made up with a collection of stuffed animals and pillows. Pointing to her collection Jane said, "My friends will just have to move over for a while." Sis looked around and up at the high ceiling.

"Gosh, this must cost a fortune to rent."

"Well, it's not too bad. The landlord inherited the house from his folks and he still lives in part of the house, but he travels a lot, so my being here gives him a feeling that the property is being looked after."

They had walked back into the center room. "Are you the only one who rents here?" Sis asked.

"No, there is another apartment but it doesn't stay rented to the same people for very long at a time. I've been here two, almost three years, so he considers me the 'old timer'. He gives me a break on the rent to keep me here." She paused, then added, "It is kind of far from the Vienna, but I don't mind."

Jane, Sis decided, was the kind of person she felt at home with from the first meeting. Though they were different in so many ways, and seemed not to have a lot in common, they shared an easy friendship from the beginning. Sis, dark in the way that Hector was, black hair straight and thick and long, her body angular and slender, contrasted with Jane's golden hair, her tall and more rounded shape.

It had been a little awkward at first, with Hector feeling so—what did it seem? "Uncomfortable," Sis thought. "Yes, that's it: he's uncomfortable with me around. I wonder if it is having me around Jane. He certainly seemed formal with her, and yet he had arranged on almost no notice for me to share her apartment. They didn't seem to be close," she thought, "but maybe they are."

"Hector with a girl friend," she mused. "Now that's something to write home about!" Sis was settling herself under the covers. When she had unpacked, she found a small package with paper and envelopes; obviously a subtle hint from her mother to write home. She began trying to write a letter in her head, telling about Hector's girlfriend, but it had been a long day, she was very tired, and sleep came right after "Dear Mama."

The next three days were busy for Sis, as she found her way around the strange city, going through the necessary steps for beginning a new job. There were orientation classes at the Civil Service headquarters, then another class at the department where she would be working. The people she met, whose names she could barely recall, all seemed nice enough, and her long walks, as she connected to the rhythm of the city, left her more tired than she would have thought. By the time Friday evening arrived she was glad of the opportunity to just get back to Jane's apartment and fall asleep. It was past eleven when she awoke to the sound of Jane coming in. She acknowledged the other girl's greeting and then slipped back into a deep sleep.

It was late the next morning when Jane awoke. Sis had made coffee and was eating when Jane came into the little kitchen. "Oh, that smells good," she said, indicating the coffee pot. Helping herself, she looked out the window at the fine day, and then turned to Sis. "Are you going to see Hector this morning?"

"I haven't talked to him since I got here," the younger girl replied. "I didn't expect him to spend all of his time with me, and I have been busy, but—well, I guess I have sort of expected him to call me."

"Sis, I see him at least twice a day, and he hasn't even asked how you're doing, so I think if you want to see him you'd better come across town with me when I go to work. He always comes in for lunch, as well as dinner."

Back again to K Street the girls went, Jane showing Sis the right electric streetcar lines to take to get from her apartment to the building where she would begin working on Monday. "You don't want to try to walk every day, especially when the weather turns hot this summer."

Jane usually arrived for her shift about ten-thirty. This morning, when she and Sis walked down K Street, Hector, on the other side of the street, was just coming out of the King of Rumania. His eyes cast down as usual, he missed them as he turned away from them. K Street is wide and usually busy, but at that hour on a Saturday it was still quiet. Sis called out, "Hector," as loudly as she could, but he continued on his way without turning around. At the corner he turned right and was gone. "He must be in a big hurry to get somewhere," Sis said after a pause.

"Or to get away from somewhere," said Jane. "Well, you could wait for him in the lobby over there, or come on in with me. He usually comes in for lunch about eleven-fifteen."

When Hector did come in, and he was almost right on the minute, Sis told herself that he hadn't seen them earlier. At least she hoped that was true. She was seated at his usual table and smiled up at him when he came and stood behind his chair. He looked at her, but it seemed to Sis that he had come to an abrupt stop because some stranger was sitting at "his" table. Then he recognized her, and his face lost its puzzled look. It was replaced almost immediately by a slight smile and then a fine little look of apology crossed his face.

"Sis," he said, quietly. "Hmm, well, uh—a nice surprise. I was wondering how you were getting on. Of course," he went on quickly, "Jane has given me a little news about your orientation classes and such—" His voice trailed off as he pulled out the chair and sat down.

Only slightly put off by Hector's breezy dismissal of his lack of interest in her, Sis momentarily found herself without a thought to tell her how to handle this conversational beginning.

"I've been pretty busy," she offered meekly. Then, "But still Hector, I am your sister. I guess I was hoping you'd be just a little concerned about what I was doing, and where I was." Her breathing was just a little fast, her heart beating rapidly. She'd never talked to her older brother like that and in fact, for the first time, she stopped thinking of him as older: just as her brother.

Taken aback, Hector looked carefully at the silverware and napkin, before looking up and into Sis's eyes. "I'm not used to entertaining family," he said in his halting, self-deprecating way.

Hector was not a very self-confident man, in spite of his experience and his age. In so many ways, Sis realized suddenly, he was still the quiet, unassuming boy who had left home nearly 15 years before.

Putting her hand out to cover his, she smiled and said, "I'm doing fine, Hector, really I am."

Chapter 7 - A Night on the Town

It's a place I come every once in a while. A lot of the customers are people I go to school with."

"When was the last time you were here?" Jane asked.

"Maybe six months," he said. "Maybe none of them will be here, but we'll see."

It was a week night, Jane's night away from the Vienna. Sis had suggested to her brother that it would be a nice gesture to invite her temporary hostess out to dinner, something Hector had never done. Probably, thought Sis, because it just would never occur to him to do something like that. By now she knew that Jane was not Hector's girlfriend, but simply the only person he knew well enough to tell he had a sister. Jane had insisted that she should pay her own way, but Hector in this at least, demonstrated his manners. "Uh, no, no. My treat."

They were at The Crystal. From his usual place behind the bar, George, in his still-thick Greek accent said "'Allo." It was clear he was surprised to see Hector, and more than that, with not just one, but two young women.

Hector acknowledged the greeting, and led the way to a booth on the right-hand side of the restaurant. They settled in and Sis looked around the room. For her this was an exotic place, the faces ranging from light to dark, the accents and languages that floated in the air strange and mysterious.

"Do you know any of these people?" she asked her brother.

Hector looked around, and nodded to a few of the others. Several of them raised a hand in greeting. Like George, their faces acknowledged that he was doing something unexpected: bringing girls with him to the restaurant.

"I know some of them. They'll probably be over in a while."

"Tell us about them." Jane was as interested in their reactions as in who they were.

"Well, see the guy over there - the one with the dark curly hair and beak nose?" He nodded to a head bobbing energetically on the other side of the double row of booths down that ran down the center of the room. "Bertrand is an assistant professor of chemistry at the university. He's French. During the war he was in the underground. He made bombs, I've heard." The girls were impressed. "And the man he is arguing with is called Henri." A darker version of Bertrand, Henri was spitting his words in rapid French. "He comes from Algeria, and he and Bertrand knew each other in the Resistance. They are constantly arguing about Algeria. Sometimes it gets very heated," he added as again the voices of Bertrand and Henri rose above the rest of the noise. "But they are very close."

"What does Henri do? Is he a professor, too?" Sis asked.

"I don't know what he does, or if he does anything. One of the guys calls him 'America's guest,' if that tells you anything."

As they watched, a tall, thin girl with long dark hair joined Bertrand and Henri. "And that is Miriam. She's from Malta. She came to the States with Henri, but I think she's Bertrand's girl now."

"Maybe that's what they are fighting about," Jane offered. The three laughed.

About this time a tall, heavily built man approached the table. He was open-faced, and friendly looking, balding prematurely, his hair wispy and uncombed. Like Hector, he wore an old, brown V-neck sweater that, in his case, emphasized his girth. "Hello, Hector," he boomed. "Where've you been?"

"Hello, Dean," Hector replied quietly. "Working, you know."

"Introduce me," Dean commanded, though in a friendly tone.

"My sister," Hector nodded to Sis, "and this is Jane. She's uh," not knowing exactly how to explain the girl, he let his voice trail off.

"Move over," Dean said, and sat down beside Hector.

"Were you in the Underground," Jane asked?

"He been telling you about the terrible two?" Dean said in response, tilting his head toward Bertrand and Henri, whose argument seemed to have run down. "No, I'm just a school teacher from a little town in West Virginia."

"Do you teach from here?" Sis asked.

"No, I'm taking a couple of years off to get some more education, thanks to Uncle Sam. Maybe find something more interesting than teaching political science to a bunch of high school students who don't want to be there anyway."

Now another pair of voices rose above the general noise level, and the four at the table turned in that direction.

"Fred and Alice still together, I see," Hector said.

"Yeah," Dean drawled. "Our West Virginia girls don't know how to be quiet."

Jane, attuned to the many different voices of the city said, "Fred doesn't sound like West Virginia."

"No, he's from Sweden." Fred was tall, about six-three, and nearly white blonde. Alice had the blonde color often found in the Appalachian country.

"Isn't he a long way from home?"

"Well," said Dean, "he came here to study the pictures in the National Gallery, which is what artists do sometimes, and met Alice and just settled in. She was getting over a divorce from a guy back home, and wanted to get as far from a West Virginia accent as she could, I guess."

"Did you know her?" Hector asked.

"Yeah, we grew up together back there." The two blondes stormed out of the restaurant, Fred in the lead, Alice still shouting threats as she followed him through the door.

"Maybe they did that to walk out without paying," Jane offered.

"Oh, no, not Fred. Money isn't a problem for that son of Sweden. He just has George send his bills to daddy. Sometimes that includes the cost of the dishes." Dean's audience laughed.

As the door swung shut, it almost immediately reopened. A dissipated-looking man carrying a trumpet case walked through the door. He was in his late thirties, with a fleshy nose, heavy lidded eyes, and thin brown hair combed straight back. Enough of it had been lost by now to give him an exaggerated widow's peak.

"Hey, man, what's happenin'" the new face asked as he came to the table. "Hey, H, you haven't made this scene in a lot of moons." Hector smiled at the pattern of speech.

"My sister, and Jane, Don. Don and I are in the same sociology class." Turning to the man, he asked, "You still making music around town?"

"Yeah, man. Just stopped by to see if anybody wanted to go down to Maynard's later. Thought I'd sit in with those cats for an hour or two."

"Oh, can we?" Sis asked. After an uncomfortable moment or two, Hector nodded.

"You like Jazz?"

"I don't know, but it sounds like fun."

37

A few hours later, sitting in the dark, smoky club on 14th Street, Sis and Jane had made themselves a part of the group. All of the faces from the restaurant, Dean, and Bertrand and Henri and Miriam, and at some point even Fred and Alice, had come in to sit and drink beer and listen to Don. On the small stage with Maynard, his brother, and the two other regulars, the trumpeter seemed in another world. His pale skin almost glowed as if in a spotlight; the dark brown faces of the other musicians a muted contrast to his own. On the solos his trumpet soared and swept the little club. When the others took their turns, Don's sound blended in naturally. For Sis this was exotic music, not at all like the juke boxes of New Rhondda, or the wheezy accordion music of her own valley.

All in all, Jane thought, it had been a successful evening. More than evening; it was nearly two in the morning when the musicians finally put away their instruments, and Don rejoined the party.

"Did you dig it, man?" he asked. The question was general, but his eyes were on the two young women. Jane, while not a frequent visitor to places like Maynard's, was at least a city girl, and a little "hip." Sis, still absorbing the atmosphere of not just the place, but the whole city, was wide-eyed and a little lost in the music. She wanted to "dig it," she knew, but so much of it was strange, so much of it new, that she was still vibrating with the beat of the jazz and could only look at Don and smile.

Dean leaned over and said, "Just nod your head, Sis. It'll make Don happy." Sis expanded her smile, nodded at Don, and then looked away.

"Time to go, ladies," Hector said. "I've got an early class tomorrow, and you," smiling at Sis, "have to work." The party stood up, and with Dean in the lead, headed out the door.

Don finished packing his trumpet, threw a quick wave to Maynard, and followed them out. The proprietor snapped the lock behind them, and the night was suddenly quieter. Hector, now marching in the lead, headed the group toward the northwest. Sis and Jane, now many blocks from the apartment, slowed down. As Hector and Don and the others moved off into the dark streets, Dean stopped, turned, and came back to the girls.

"Let's find a cab," he offered. "Not too many out at this time of night in the middle of the week, but there should be one or two still about."

As the trio approached Pennsylvania Avenue, near the National Theater, a single cab pulled into the stand. They were soon on their way to Jane's apartment, Dean comfortably between the two young women. At the apartment Dean had the driver wait, while he saw them to the door.

"Now I'll know where to find you," he said with a smile directed at Sis. The girls wished him good night, and he returned to the cab.

"Dean's such a gentleman," Sis remarked.

"Well," Jane opened the door and, after a long pause, said: "Hector is Hector." The door closed behind them.

Chapter 8 - In Time of War

Hector had started talking to Jane when she came to clear away the dishes in front of him. He asked for another cup of coffee, something he rarely did. Jane had brought it, and because it was a slow time, stood by the table and launched a conversation.

"Sis seems to be enjoying her new job," she offered, glancing at Hector in the mirror. His gaze, which had been aimless, focused on her there.

"Is she?" Hector wasn't seeing his sister as she was now.

"She's sure grown," he said. "You know, when I left home she was just a baby -- eight or nine at the most."

Jane picked up the empty dessert plate and walked back to the service area. In her mind she tried to picture not the attractive 24-year old who was sharing her apartment, but rather a child who could be Hector's sister, and along with that image, a much younger Hector. She shook her head. The image of Sis was easy enough, but Hector—that was different. Surely he was thinner, gangly perhaps, but she felt certain he was no easier to know than he was now. "A loner," she thought, "scared of girls." The picture enlarged: a boy of middle height, loose jointed, unruly hair, eyes that told nothing, timid and quiet.

Jane was busy with a flurry of customers, and it was some time before she realized that Hector was still at his table, still sipping what must have been lukewarm if not cold coffee. When she looked at him he was slowly writing something on his pad, looking up absently in the mirror from time to time. She left him alone, taking care of her other tables, delivering and busing and refilling and preparing checks. By nine the crowd was gone, the restaurant gradually slowing to a typical week night tempo. She wondered what was going on in Hector's life that had brought so great a change in his daily habit. He was not a late diner usually, and she had seldom seen him after seven-thirty or so, unless he was with Sis. "And that is almost never," she said half aloud.

Her curiosity aroused, Jane brought the coffee pot to Hector's table and poured without asking. He looked up, again in the mirror, and smiled his gentle slow smile. "Umm, yes," was all he said, but his eyes, she noted, were actually focused on her image. Then he turned to look at her directly. "I hope I'm not keeping the table from someone else."

Jane continued to look at him in the mirror.

"No, this is your table, you know. Valery says we have to treat our regulars 'special'." She gave the words a little smile. "Just don't keep us here after closing," she added, still smiling. "Looks like you're working."

In the short time since Sis had moved into Jane and Hector's lives, Jane had learned that Hector was working on a book. She had no idea what kind, or what it was about, but she liked the idea that she knew someone who could attempt something so beyond her own experience.

"You're writing a novel?" she ventured. Hector nodded. "What's it about?"

"People, mostly." He said nothing more, but turned back to his notebook.

"That's exciting." When nothing followed, Jane walked away.

By ten the restaurant had emptied, and Jane had only Hector's table to finish. Instead, she pulled out one of the chairs and sat down. Hector turned his head to look at the girl.

"Sorry," he said quietly. "I'll get going." He began to close his notebook and put his pen in his pocket. "I just felt I wanted to be around people tonight." The words were flat, smoothly connected, not emotional at all.

"Is tonight special?"

"Yeah, kind of. It's a long story." Jane wasn't sure whether she sensed a need in him to talk, or if it was only her own curiosity, but she led with the obvious,

"Can you tell it to me?"

Hector's response was quick, almost abrupt, "No." Not emphatic, simply short. "No." Then he said, "I'm afraid it would take a long time."

He looked up in the mirror, saw a couple sitting at a table. A man neither young nor old, a girl with regular features and an attractive smile. Their eyes met in the mirror.

"If you have time, I could try," he said slowly.

"Just let me finish here and if you still want to, you can tell me on the way home." Jane couldn't believe her own voice had spoken those words of invitation, but as she listened to them again she realized they sounded right.

The streetcar hummed and rattled along the rails, the contact shoe occasionally screeching in the open third rail. Hector and Jane were sitting on one of the side-facing seats, rocking with the sway of the car as it rolled east toward her neighborhood. For a long time Hector had said very little, after saying that he had been thinking about the war, that this was the anniversary of the night when he had left home to join the army so many years ago. Opposite, the night-darkened glass reflected the two travelers, their eyes meeting briefly, but his not really seeing. He was looking into another night, a long night in his past.

"When you are 16 or 17, and your country is at war," Hector was saying, "it all seems so glamorous, so exciting, and at the same time, scary." Another long pause, then: "I finished school in the middle of the year, and needed to go to work. The war was on, and it was that or the mine, so I chose the war. That's how it was, at least for me. I knew I'd be drafted soon anyway, so I just went and signed up." He rested again. The metal wheels of the car sang, the warning gong clanged, and the capsule rocked on across the city. "Even if the war had been over, I probably would have done the same thing. I didn't want to go into the mine." Again silence.

Jane reflected on her own escape from home, though it was just across the river in a small village beyond Arlington, hardly more than a crossroads, and nodded her head in understanding.

"I couldn't wait to get away from home, either," she said. "Not that there was anything wrong. I just wanted to be on my own. I'm glad I did it."

Hector looked directly at her reflection. "Oh, I'm not sorry I left," he said, the inflection in his voice rising. "Whatever happened, I knew it had to be better than the mines." A short silence, and then he began a story that would continue after the two left the streetcar to walk to Jane's apartment.

The story he told was not unusual for his age and time. In the army he had completed basic training, then had been selected for clerk school. He learned to type, to file, to fill in forms and make reports for his sergeant or the lieutenant to sign. He was very good at the work, and so he remained at the training center, attached to the headquarters staff. When the war was over, without enough points for discharge, he was sent to a replacement depot. From there he was assigned to an infantry unit for occupation duty in Japan.

"I liked being in a foreign country, being far enough away from home to not even think about going back to it."

It was a devastated country, but he had been assigned to an infantry unit stationed at Zama, near Tokyo. His camp had been an officer cadet training center, with permanent buildings for both offices and barracks. As the local rail transportation system was reestablished Hector, like so many others, took passes to visit cities and villages around the main island.

"After a while it wasn't so foreign. Some of the countryside even looked a little like Pennsylvania, near where I came from. All in all," Hector said, "it had been a good time."

Jane sat quietly beside the young man, thinking how animated he had become as he told the story. From time to time he even looked at her, his expression questioning whether or not he should go on with the narrative. In response Jane would nod, or smile and, on occasion, say something encouraging. But he really didn't seem to need that. The act of beginning the story had, somehow, unlocked a need he hadn't before realized, to share the experience with someone.

Even though most of the men in his division were eventually sent home, Hector remained in the Far East. When he was offered the chance to reenlist, he accepted and stayed on in Japan. Soon he was promoted and reassigned to Tokyo. He was a good soldier. He lived in a barracks, ate in a mess hall, and only occasionally went out into the reawakening city. What friends he had were neither carousers nor curious. Quiet men, occasionally visiting a local restaurant or bar, but mostly just living on an army compound, on army pay, as they would have in Alabama or New Jersey or North Carolina. A peacetime army, with peacetime activities, different only because it was a few thousand miles away from home. A corporal now, Hector worked in a big office with other clerks, doing a not very demanding job, suited to his nature.

Less than two years into his second enlistment, all of that changed. And it changed as much for Hector as for anyone. It was June, 1950, and soldiers from North Korea had crossed the 38th Parallel headed for Seoul. The first commitment of American troops would come shortly.

It wasn't particularly cold, especially in the headquarters tent. They were back of what was a very narrow front line, below the crest of the hill. It had just grown dark, but the sergeant, the tent's only occupant at this hour, was typing a report. The officers were in their hootch not far away, and Hector, occasionally sipping coffee from his canteen cup, was taking his time. Outside there were intermittent pops of rifle fire, and from time to time the wall of the tent would glow from the light of an aerial flare. At irregular intervals a howitzer, somewhere behind the company area, would send a shell whistling overhead toward an unseen target. He hardly noticed the short thumps, and only vaguely recorded the slight lifting of the ground beneath him as the high explosive charges responded to the gunner's lanyard.

"What the hell—" "Look out—gooks!" "Jesus.." Shouts and shots suddenly erupted just beyond the tent. Drums, whistles, bugles blown off-key shot through the October air. A machine gun began to rattle, a grenade made a "clump" sound, a voice screamed in pain.

His attention suddenly redirected, Hector looked up, then jumped up as the tent flap was whipped aside. The face on top of the uniform was not his CO's, was not anyone he knew, was certainly not an American. "No, not me," he heard himself shout, falling involuntarily over the upset canvas stool. The enemy advanced into the tent, momentarily blinded by the bright gas lantern on a wire above Hector's olive green desk. In that split second of fear and falling, Hector's hand fell on his M-1 where it lay on the floor. In one motion he grabbed it up, found the safety, and pulled the trigger. The semi-automatic weapon fired three, maybe four times, the recoil raising the rifle higher with each shot. His startled attacker fell back, dropped his own weapon, and died.

With the adrenalin coursing through him, Hector scrambled to his feet, feeling the power that was so new to him, responding to forces he didn't know existed, knocked over the bullet scarred desk, leaped over the prostrate enemy, and still shouting "No! Not me!" over and over, he rushed out and unloaded his rifle into the body of someone rushing toward him. Falling, the enemy soldier dropped his machine pistol at Hector's feet. Throwing down his own empty rifle, Hector scooped up the unfamiliar weapon, found the trigger and began filling the night with Chinese-made bullets.

The light coming through the hospital tent wall was subdued and overshadowed by the feeble electric lights strung down the middle. Hector was only vaguely aware of being in a hazy somewhere, of feeling disconnected from himself, of distant sounds. The lights, driven by a humming generator not far away, occasionally flickered, dimming and brightening, much as his own consciousness came and went. He slept. He woke, feeling pain he hadn't remembered. He slept. He heard a voice far away shouting, "No! Not me! No! Not me!" He felt the warmth of morphine overtake him again and he slept.

Three days after the attack, Hector was recovering on the open ward. He still had little recollection of the fighting, and none at all of his role in the engagement. It had been brief, it had been intense, but all he could remember was pain and the voices and lights of the surgical tent, and the coming and going of consciousness. Today was better. He did not feel deep, searing pain, and his thoughts seemed more coherent, less episodic. A nurse, a lieutenant in the khaki uniform of the front line hospitals, was checking his IV.

"Pain still with you, soldier?" she asked gently.

"Some, ma'am, mostly in my shoulder."

"Time to find out how long you can go without this, then" she said, putting the morphine syringe back on her tray. "Let me know if the pain gets too bad." She busied herself with his position on the cot, and then turned away. "You'll want to be alert this afternoon. Your regimental commander is coming to see you." Pulling the privacy drape out of the way, she left him and went to her next patient.

Hector closed his eyes. No question entered his mind, no curiosity about what the colonel's visit could mean, no speculation interrupted his thoughts. Nor did he spend much time thinking about what had happened to bring him to the hospital. He knew he hurt, surmised he had been wounded, but was content to simply lie back and wait. Whatever had happened was over, and he was alive.

"An amazing bit of shooting for a clerk!" It was late in the afternoon, and the colonel, along with Hector's commanding officer and another officer he knew only by sight, were ranged around the cot. Hector had been propped up by the nurse and a corpsman, but even that effort had tired him. The other officers nodded in agreement.

"Been looking at your files, Collin, and I can't even find an expert marksmanship badge in your record." Hector had qualified as he had to, but being a clerk, there wasn't much pressure to exceed the minimum.

The lieutenant turned to Hector. "If it hadn't been for what you did, I think the whole headquarters would have been lost."

Hector, deep in his head, heard a voice saying, "No, no. Not me. Not me."

"Must have gotten five or six of the gooks," the officer continued.

"No, no! Not me! Not me!"

"A real hero," said the colonel.

"No, no! Not me! Not me!"

"Just wanted to see the man in my regiment who could do that and still be alive," the colonel said.

"No, no! Not me! Not me!"

The words kept repeating in Hector's mind.

"Just stood there and emptied one weapon, then picked up one from the second or third guy he killed, and kept on shooting," the lieutenant said.

"No, no! Not me! Not me!"

A photographer stood at the end of the bed, holding his SpeedGraphic with one hand, the flashgun detached from the case in the other. The bulb flashed, he pushed in the slide, flipped the film holder over and put in another bulb.

"Sir, if you and the captain could stand on either side of the bed, it would make a good picture," the PFC said. The two men moved into position, the major moving out of range. The colonel, accustomed to his photographer's directions, placed a hand on Hector's uninjured shoulder, and looked down at the young man. The lieutenant stood stiffly at ease.

Hector and Jane had stopped walking and stood on the sidewalk in front of the building where she lived. "The thing is," he was saying, "I really didn't remember what had happened. I couldn't believe it was me they were talking about." He paused, looked up at the sky, then down at the ground. "I thought I had done something wrong when I saw those three men coming to my cot. When they began talking about what I had done, I knew it was something terrible. Then it finally dawned on me that they thought I was some kind of hero, that I had done something you read about in history books. I knew it wasn't me."

The rest of that afternoon, Hector told Jane, he was sure they would come back and tell him they had made a mistake. That he wasn't the soldier they were looking for. Slowly, though, the action buried in his mind grew into focused images. He saw himself, remembered the attack, the enemy soldier breaking into the tent. In excruciatingly slow motion he watched himself, saw his hand fall on his rifle, relived the feeling of his arms weighed down with what felt like tons of lead, felt the recoil of the rifle as he fired from the floor. Yes he had gotten up, yes he had stepped over the dead soldier, and yes, yes, he had pushed his way outside, still holding the rifle, still moving as if he wore chains, only to confront yet another screaming enemy. He saw him go down, felt his rifle kick then stop, knew he was out of ammunition. In the swirl of motion and the awful concert of screams and explosions he watched other soldiers die from the fire of the weapon he had picked up from the ground. The only time the action seemed to speed up was when the first bullet tore into him. After that time ran faster. He felt the tug of a second impact, and then a third, before he crumpled to the ground. And through it all, he heard his voice, tearful, frightened, screaming, "No, no! Not me! Not me!"

"I'm not a hero," he told Jane. "I'm not. Not me"

Chapter 9 - Sis

Jane woke up the next morning to find Sis still in the apartment. As she turned over and looked out the door to the middle room, Sis walked in, still in her pajamas, holding a cup of coffee. Coming over to the bed, she handed the cup to Jane.

"I heard you and Hector talking out front last night," she said with a smile. "How did you get him to walk you home?"

Jane laughed and took the cup. After a sip she replied: "He wanted to talk, and even stayed in the restaurant until we closed. I wanted to get home, and the only way to let him talk was to invite him to bring me." Both girls laughed, as much at the idea of Hector wanting to talk, as at Jane suggesting he accompany her home.

"And what are you doing still here at this hour?" Jane asked.

"It's Saturday, Jane," Sis said with a laugh. "Did your 'date' with Hector make you forget what day it is?" Jane said something under her breath, and got up.

"But what did you talk about?" Sis was following Jane around as the older girl prepared to leave for work.

Jane's reply was thoughtful. "He wanted to talk about the war. He sounds like a real hero."

"Hector? A hero?" Sis was obviously surprised. "When? All I ever knew was that he joined the army and then, about three or four years ago, I guess, he was here in Washington, going to college."

"You mean he never wrote about it in his letters home?" Jane was about to leave. She turned as she opened the door, and said: "Maybe your folks thought you shouldn't know."

"Oh, no," Sis said. "I don't think there was one letter from my brother the whole time he was in the army, except to tell us he was getting out and going to college." Jane looked at the young girl, and saw a mixture of consternation and hero worship on her face. "And the only reason he wrote that much, I guess, was to let us know the monthly allotment would end when he was discharged."

"Allotment?"

"A portion of his army pay that he sent home every month." Sis told Jane about going to the university with that money.

"Oh, that was so nice of him."

"In our valley, that's what older brothers and sisters do," Sis said. Jane walked through the door and down the stairs. Sis remained in the doorway, gazing thoughtfully after her roommate.

When Hector came in for lunch, Sis was with him. They went to his table and sat, obviously continuing a conversation they had started before coming in. Jane walked over and offered Sis a menu, but said nothing. Sis continued to look at her brother, and Hector continued to talk in his unemotional, slow way. Jane realized he was repeating some of what she had heard the night before. She left them and went to take care of her other tables.

"Hector, why haven't you told anybody about this before?" Sis asked. "Daddy would be so proud of you."

"I—I don't think they'd understand, Sis. And neither would you," he said, looking away. His eyes didn't search the mirror, but simply stared into a corner of the room. "All of that 'hero' stuff is—well, it's just stuff." His voice trailed off.

"Did they give you a medal?" Sis continued to pursue him.

"Look, Sis, everybody got medals. It wasn't anything special. Besides, they wanted me to go home and talk about it, and I just couldn't. It was a one-time thing. I was scared, and I guess I was just trying to save myself."

Even before he was issued a new uniform, there were medals. Finally, when he was allowed to leave the hospital, he was ordered back to the States to finish his recuperation. This time, when his enlistment was up, he didn't even consider another tour. "I think it's time I got out," he told the reenlistment sergeant. "I want to go to college."

All during his rehabilitation at Walter Reed, the big army hospital in Washington, Hector had thought about what he wanted to do, and where. The several colleges and universities in the city offered more than enough choices. Washington was a comfortable place for him, after the exaggerated atmosphere of Tokyo.

Hector sensed he could lose himself in a city, and in a university already used to returning servicemen and women, taking advantage of their country's generosity. Unlike many of his classmates, though, Hector put away his army issue and adopted his new uniform of corduroys, open-necked dress shirt, and sweater. He faded into the veteran-filled landscape, unremarkable because that was how he wanted to be. He wanted to be unseen.

The university, for Hector, was a kind of finishing school. His knowledge of the world was circumscribed by his experiences, and his universe was at best a shallow place. With no clear direction in mind, he had taken the courses the university required, eventually finding himself with enough credits to graduate in the coming spring. Not exactly prepared for anything, Hector was in possession of enough knowledge to at least be able to see the world in which he lived.

"Understanding of it," one of his professors had always said, "would come with experience and age." How much more experience, at what age, were questions Hector only vaguely considered. They were the kinds of questions younger students discussed in dormitory "bull sessions" late at night.

If he thought about the future, Hector knew, he would have to confront the past. For now he was comfortable just going from day to day, dealing only with the routine and the mundane. Even his novel was a series of snapshots of today. Whatever of himself he put into it, it was not about the warrior and the war.

He had started the story as part of a creative writing class assignment. Professor Enders was an elderly, pedantic, but gracious teacher. A wreath of white hair framed a lined face, and an equally white moustache covered the space above his lips. When he spoke about writers and writing, he generated an enthusiasm even in Hector. To perform well in that class became almost an obsession with the younger man.

Enders encouraged his students to look within themselves for the raw material of fiction. For Hector the look only encompassed his present, never penetrating his past. He began simply enough, with a story about an older freshman in classes with so many younger people, boys and girls, really, not yet "men and women." He focused the story in such a way, professor Enders had commented, that a reader would not know or even question why a man of thirty would just be starting college. It was simply a story of a man of experience coming into contact with a world he had never known, reacting to it as if he had never faced life at all.

Even Hector had been surprised at the analysis; he had simply tried to tell the story of a man a little confused by exposure to a new world. The notes and discussion of his work in the classroom encouraged him to go on with the story. He found, sitting at his typewriter in his solitary room, that he had so many words, so many thoughts and impressions that he wanted to see on paper, that the writing was almost effortless at the beginning.

When Hector was writing, everything else seemed to recede into the background. In the beginning he worried about where the words would come from, but as he accepted the voice within, the words found their way out onto the page. When he was writing he felt, for the first time, comfortable and at home. As a sentence or a paragraph laid itself down on the paper, he felt an inner fire that he had seldom known. Watching the pages grow in number didn't impress him, but an individual story, or a single line, could bring him great pleasure. Hector, it seemed, had found his role in life. By his own choice he would try to be a chronicler of his generation.

Chapter 10 - Dean

There's a concert tonight at the Watergate," Dean said. "Would you like to go?" It took Sis a second to put a name and face to the voice, but the West Virginia drawl quickly recalled the rumpled former teacher Hector had introduced her to at The Crystal a month before.

"How did you find me?" the girl asked.

"Oh, I went by the restaurant and asked Jane," he replied. "So do you want to go to the Watergate concert?"

"What's a Watergate?" Sis responded. "Sounds like something a plumber does."

Dean laughed. "The Watergate, my country bumpkin, is a barge with a band shell on it. It is anchored in the Potomac, near the brewery. The military bands play there this time of year."

"Oh, what are they playing?" Sis's musical education had already been expanded by the music she had heard at Maynard's. She hoped it would be like that.

"Well, tonight is the annual performance of the 1812 Overture, you know, the one that goes dada-dada-dada da-da-boom!"

"I'm afraid I don't," Sis said.

"Well, anyway, the Army Band will be playing, and they use real cannon for the boom," Dean laughed. "I'll come by about six and we can take the streetcar over."

The K Street line had deposited the couple a short walk from where the barge was moored. On the ride across town Dean had talked more about the music, about Tchaikovsky, and about the war the Russians and the French had fought in the early years of the 19th century. Sis knew a lot about that war, Dean discovered. Russian history had been her college major, and that increased his growing interest in the young woman.

They settled themselves on the steps leading down to the water, and watched as the band members crossed the wooden gangplank and began to arrange themselves for the performance. In the crowd that was gathering were several people Sis recognized from the night she and Jane had gone with Hector to the jazz club on 14th Street, and Dean refreshed her memory by putting names to the faces.

"Does Hector ever come to the um, Watergate?" she asked.

"I don't think he's much interested in music, Sis," her escort responded. "I'm not really sure what he's interested in. Is it Jane?"

Sis laughed. "Well, it might be, Dean. How well do you know my brother?"

Dean hesitated a moment before answering. "To tell you the truth, Sis, I really only know him from class, the creative writing class with Dr. Enders, and from the times he has shown up at The Crystal. He keeps pretty much to himself."

Sis had to smile at Dean's last description. "He does that," she said. "Does he ever talk about his time in the army?"

"No." Dean was thoughtful. "Most of us don't, you know. In a way we all shared the experience, whether we were in the fighting or not, and there really isn't that much to say." He paused again. "No, I think most of us just want to go on with our lives."

Dean turned toward the bandstand as the loudspeakers came to life and the announcer, a sergeant, introduced the conductor and the program. Conversations trailed off and ended as the announcer said, "Ladies and gentlemen, our National Anthem." The audience rose, and Sis saw that a lot of the young men and women stood at attention as the music began to roll out from the band shell.

Excited and exhausted by the power and the sound of the mighty overture, with the ground-shaking cannon fire punctuating the final movement, Sis rose slowly as the crowd began to leave the steps.

"Something, isn't it?" Dean asked, taking her elbow to guide her up to the street.

"I've never heard anything like that," Sis said. Her voice was quiet, her emotions still attenuated by the music. "Are all the concerts here like that?"

"No, not all. Sometimes it's show tunes, sometimes dance music. Depends on the program. But it's always good. We'll come again, if you'd like."

"Oh, yes, please." For a while they walked on in silence.

They were standing on the streetcar platform in the middle of K Street, waiting for a car to take them back across town.

"Dean, did everybody get medals in the army?"

"Well, yes, I guess so. At least a good conduct medal, and a service ribbon showing where you were if you were overseas. Things like that."

"How can you find out if someone got more than that? Something for being a hero?" Dean looked at the young woman beside him. Her interest wasn't focused on him, he knew.

At that moment the green streetcar arrived and stopped for them to board. Once settled in their seats, Sis repeated the question.

"You talking about Hector?" Dean asked. "Well, I don't guess it would do any good to ask him, would it?"

Sis smiled up at the man beside her, and shook her head.

"Why do you think he has medals?"

"He told Jane about it." Dean looked at the girl speculatively.

"He never told you about it?"

"Not until after he talked to Jane one night about a week ago. She told me a little, and then I asked him to tell me all of it."

"Did he?"

"Well, that's just what I don't know, Dean," the girl said. "That's why I'd like to know for sure. Daddy would be so proud to know what Hector had done."

Even as she said it, Sis wondered if Daddy would ever say he was proud, or that he cared. Theirs wasn't a demonstrative family, though she never questioned her parents' love. Not for her, not for Hector, not for each other. But certainly it wasn't something the coal miner let shine through from his dark world. For the first time, Sis considered her father and mother as people, and saw in Hector a true reflection of them. Was she like that, too? Dean, large, friendly, outgoing, seemed almost soft to her. How did she appear to him, she wondered.

They made an interesting pair: Sis, slender and neat, about medium height, skin fair and hair very dark; Dean, tall, rumpled, a little paunchy, hair thinning, looking a bit older than the thirty-six he was. His face, creased by smile lines, wore a pleasant, if private, expression.

As they walked the few blocks to the apartment they kept what Mrs. Collin would have called a 'proper distance' apart. By the time they reached the door, the separation had decreased, and their arms almost touched.

At the street door Sis turned to Dean. For an instant there seemed to be a charge between them, but then Sis shook her head, stepped back a half-step, and offered her hand. Dean took it graciously, and with a slight squeeze, they parted.

As she went through the door Sis turned and said, "Thanks, Dean. I really enjoyed the music, and the talk."

"How about next week?" Dean asked.

"Maybe," Sis replied. "Yes, that might be nice. In the meantime, if you figure out how I can learn more about Hector, please call me. Please call me anyway," she ended. She turned and let the door close as Dean headed back to the center of the city.

Chapter 11 - Hector Calls

Summer in Washington seldom ends with a noticeable signature. It just slowly fades into Fall. This year was no exception. August, the rainy month, the humid, paper-curling, sleep-depriving precursor was no surprise, and no delight. It was simply August. And then, with nothing more remarkable than the changing of a calendar page, September began.

Hector, sitting at the small desk before the window, was aware of little beyond the clacking keys of his typewriter. The sound was a white noise that isolated him from all but his own thoughts. The manuscript now stood at 350 pages. The story was told, and the writer was now the editor, working his way through it page by page, refining, removing, reworking lines and paragraphs, pages and chapters. It was now that he began to recognize the effort as work, not the wrenching cathartic that had possessed him as he pounded out the first draft.

From time to time he saw himself as if from a place on the ceiling, and wondered at this man he didn't really know. Head and shoulders bent over the typewriter, a sense of purpose in his energy, the man seemed wedded to his machine much as a woodworker embraces his tools. Nowhere in his mind was there a question about why he was doing what he was, or what he hoped to accomplish by his labor. It was simply his job, and he approached it with the same effort and attention to detail he had brought to his military assignments, and later to his college classes.

With the help of Professor Enders, Hector had begun sending out sample chapters and query letters to agents known to the older man. The replies were cordial and encouraging.

On the first Tuesday in September, a letter came from Margery Maxwell, an agent in New York. When he had come down the stairs on his way to lunch, the gold earrings in Mary McAllister's ears were visibly vibrating as she called Hector's name.

"Oh Mr. Collin," her voice strode across the dim lobby, "A letter from New York for you." As he had the day Sis's letter arrived, Hector reacted with not much more than a nod of his head. Taking the letter, he continued out the door, headed for the Vienna.

Though he sat at his regular table, Jane was not there to serve him. She had taken the Labor Day weekend and the rest of the week to visit her parents, now living in Florida. Valery substituted for her absent employee, and really, it wasn't too difficult. This was usually the slowest week of the year for the Vienna.

In the past Hector would hardly have noticed Jane's absence, or Valery's presence for that matter. But the letter he read was itself a change from the past.

"Dear Mr. Collin," it began. "I will be in Washington next week for a few days. I would like very much to discuss your book with you. I have shown the first five chapters to an editor at Doubleday, and I believe they are giving it serious consideration. Could we meet at Paul Potter's bookshop on Thursday afternoon?" Hector's hands began to perspire. An agent with an offer! He looked up, scanning the mirror for Jane, before he remembered she was not in the restaurant.

Sis held the phone slightly away from her ear. It took a moment for her to associate the excited, slightly breathless voice with her brother, but Hector it was, and the excitement was real.

"Sis," Hector finally was able to say, "an agent thinks she has a contract for my book!" The small phone booth across from the desk in the King of Rumania lobby was, despite the whirring vent fan, warm and suffocating. The smell of the aged wood, plus years of accumulated cigarette and cigar smoke, triggered the need for air, and every breath was difficult.

Without saying more, Hector hung the receiver on the worn black metal hook, and opened the folding door. He neither saw nor heard Mary McAllister as he walked slowly past her. She leaned far forward across the counter, but failed to catch his eye.

At the sidewalk, Hector turned to the left and began walking toward Connecticut Avenue. At 17th Street he turned south, toward the river, walking slowly, without purpose, but maintaining a steady gait. One foot lifted, one foot took the weight, over and over, pausing only to avoid the traffic flowing across his path. After perhaps twenty minutes he arrived at the curving walkway along the Tidal Basin. Resting his forearms on the round guard rail, Hector leaned forward, looking down at the moving water. As the wavelets splashed against the retaining wall, then moved back toward center, so did his thoughts. A publisher for his book. College nearly completed. No home. No going back to yesterday. What future? His reflection in the dark water twisted and bent with the action of the tide coming or going, he didn't know which. Was he on the way in or out? Where was his life going? Too many questions flooded his mind. Too many options, but none he could identify. Would he become a famous author, or was this going to be just an isolated, one-time success? Were these doubts that assailed him the ones unexpected success conjured in anyone? Was this real? Had he really written a book worthy of being published? "No, not me!" rang again in his head.

The early sunset of a September evening cast Hector's shadow backward onto the grass behind him. He was still at the railing, still watching the movement of the water, seeing the slowly rising tide against the wall at his feet, but curiously, for a long time, his mind had been empty of any recollected thoughts. As he raised his eyes from the water the after-image of the flickering wave tops momentarily obscured his vision, and he blinked rapidly. He looked at the watch on his wrist and realized it was nearly seven o'clock. Turning, he put his back against the rail and let his eyes readjust, looking in the distance at the yellow light on the white buildings of the city that rose and spread before him. The late sun warmed his back, but still he noted a chill inside. Where had the afternoon gone? Where was he going?

With a faster gait he began walking back toward Dupont Circle. As he walked, the noises of the city began to infiltrate his consciousness once again. As awareness returned, his steps quickened to his normal pace, as if he marched to a band only he could hear. He had no particular destination in mind, when he found himself in front of the Crystal. Suddenly his mood switched again, stopping him from entering. Should he go in and see if any of the usual gang were there to hear the news? What if it didn't work out? Suppose this was just a form letter. No, it was too personalized. Should he tell anyone else? He was almost sorry he had called Sis. Surely she would tell the family back home. And Dean. She was seeing him a lot lately, he thought. Turning abruptly away from the door, he began walking west, toward K Street again. He would wait until he had met the agent from New York. But could he wait that long? He turned again toward the restaurant, hesitated, turned again on his heel and continued back toward the King of Rumania.

Thursday Hector was up before daylight, unable to sleep. His meeting with the agent was not until the afternoon, but he was already anticipating the conversation. Yesterday, the day after he had received the letter from Miss Maxwell, Hector had finally sought out Professor Enders.

In the small office the older man maintained on the campus, books and student manuscripts fought for space on the desk and institutional bookshelves. Picturing his own almost compulsively neat desk, Hector wondered if this was where his mentor wrote his own books and short stories. In his gentle, low key manner Enders encouraged Hector to accept the letter at face value. The agent, he assured the younger man, was a good judge of both writers and publishers. Hector left the office feeling a bit more assured about the coming meeting, but still not at ease with the prospect of success.

With the morning before him, Hector turned to his desk and the typescript. Unlike other days, the steps of reading the previous day's work, and beginning where he had left off did not hold his attention. His thoughts kept returning to his coming interview. What would happen, he wondered, if the book really did get published? The idea of other people, strangers, reading his words, his story, suddenly leapt into his mind. They couldn't know anything about what he really felt, he knew. They surely would find him pretentious, a word Enders often used to describe what he termed "upstart scribblers." Of course he was one of those, Hector thought. Enders was simply leading him on. No, he wouldn't do that. Yes he would. Soon the young man's mind was in a spiral leading down into a dark and dangerous place. "No, no! Not me!" The words ran like background music in his mind.

A warm, damp breeze moved slowly up 7th Street toward the public library. As it passed the narrow doorway of the old bookshop, it brushed an equally warm and damp Hector, just a few minutes early for his appointment with the agent. As he entered the dark shop he saw Potter sitting in one of the old easy chairs near the cash register. In the companion chair was a slender woman of elegant stature and indeterminate age. As the rumpled young man made his way down the crowded aisle the woman looked at him. Her face smiled and she began to rise. Potter, older, comfortable with his weight, the quintessential antiquarian book man, rose more slowly, as Margery said, "I believe this is the young man I was telling you about, Paul."

Shifting the box containing the manuscript from his right to his left hand, Hector extended, then withdrew then extended again the now empty hand. The woman touched it only briefly before dropping her own to her side. "Please sit down, Mr. Collin," indicating the chair where Potter had been sitting. Hector looked at the other man, who smiled and returned to the front of his store. The younger man waited until the woman had sat down, and then lowered himself into the soft chair. He looked expectantly at Miss Maxwell. So far he had not said a word. The woman smiled at him and waited. When he said nothing, she pulled the box toward her, saying, "Is it complete?"

Hector cleared his throat; it was dry and constricted and swallowing didn't seem to help. Finally he nodded and said, rather shakily, "I've been rewriting it for the past month. To make it smoother." He looked away.

For the next three hours he sat opposite the sophisticated lady from New York, watching her as she devoured the pages she took from the box. Her eyes never moved from the page, so intense was her concentration. Finally, turning the last page into the upturned boxtop, she closed her eyes briefly, resting them he realized, then looked at him and smiled.

"Well done, Mr. Collin. Well done."

Chapter 12 - Response

The city Jane returned to at the end of her vacation was not the city she had left. The summer heat remained, but the hint of Fall was in the evening air. Windows in the un-airconditioned apartments opened to welcome the breeze coming off the river as the sun slanted down the broad streets.

Sis could barely contain herself as she related the news. Hector, it seemed, was truly going to have his book published. When it would happen, or how, was as much a mystery to the two girls as to Hector himself. He seemed somewhat bewildered by the sudden turn his life was taking, but with it all he remained the quiet, contained man he had always been.

Jane was in the Vienna for the first time since her vacation when Hector came in for lunch. She saw only a slight change in him. Standing in the shadows near the window to the kitchen, Jane watched the man come quietly, almost silently across the tiled floor to his table. He looked around only briefly, not seeing Jane, before he sat down. He seemed, she thought, to sit a little more rigidly in his chair, seemed drawn more tightly into himself. From his shirt pocket he fished out the small notebook he always carried, and put it on the table. From the same pocket he pulled the Parker fountain pen and placed it beside the notebook. He stared for a moment at the pen, and a quick smile crossed his face. The pen was a gift he had given himself years ago, purchased in the PX. "A fine tool for a clerk," he had thought at the time. Now it represented a badge of the writer's craft.

"The pen," Jane thought, "is what separates us. Separates him from all of us." The image of Hector wielding a pen like a sword, not to defend himself, but to fend off interruption, flickered across her mind's eye. "Not interruption," she thought, reconsidering the word. "Intrusion. Yes, that's it. Hector seems so afraid of letting any of us into his life. Maybe that's why his book is about other people." She and Sis had often talked about the wall Hector seemed to keep tightly around himself. "Now," Jane thought, "the wall will never come down. And I will never be able to get over it."

As she walked toward Hector, Jane suddenly realized what her words meant. Somehow, without intending to, she had become attracted to this quiet, often diffident, always obscured personality, this stranger who was her friend, who was a hero and afraid, who was a man she wanted to care for her.

Holding out a menu, Jane said, "Nothing's changed—on the menu, I mean. Do you want to look anyway?"

Hector looked up from his notebook, his face presenting just a flicker of a smile, and said slowly, "Hello, Jane. How was Florida?"

"Hot and humid," she replied, "just like here."

"I've never been to Florida," he said.

"Well, now you can go if you want to, can't you?" Jane hadn't meant to sound brittle, but that is the way the words came out.

"I'm glad you're back," Hector said.

The rest of the day was very busy for Jane. The restaurant seemed more full that evening, and at some point she realized that Hector was taking longer than usual to eat dinner. In fact, she noticed, he was still sitting at his table when all the other customers had gone. As she cleared another table, her back to him, she heard him speak her name. His voice had a little more volume than usual, but it was still his voice.

"Jane," he said again, "may I see you home tonight?"

Her heart beat an extra beat at the question. She paused for a second, hoping the smile on her face wouldn't be too eager, then she turned and looked at him.

"I'd like that," her voice had just a touch of tightness to it.

"I'll just wait here, then," he said.

Jane quickly cleared his table, and hurried through her closing routine. In less than fifteen minutes they were walking toward the streetcar stop.

The big green and cream car clanked and screeched to a stop as Hector and Jane prepared to get off. On the trip across town he had been more quiet than the girl had expected, but Hector wasn't ready to begin a conversation on the noisy, swaying car, she thought.

Hector left the car first, then turned to offer Jane his hand as she stepped onto the platform. Taking it, she noticed its warmth, and felt a slight pressure as his fingers wrapped around her hand. For the several blocks they walked, he did not let it go.

Stepping off the platform and crossing to the sidewalk, Hector began to speak. "I haven't told many people about my book," he began. "I don't know what will happen, and I guess I don't want to be a failure. For the first time, Jane, I'm afraid of failing. But for the first time, I have something to fail at," he let his voice trail off. Before Jane could say anything, he continued: "You know, when you asked me what my book was about, I didn't know exactly how to tell you. Now that it's finished I understand better what I've been doing."

Again Jane waited for Hector to go on.

The couple crossed the street at the intersection and turned toward the river. Looking up at the night sky, Hector said, "The stars are hard to see in the city. Sometimes you can't see them at all." He paused before returning to his original subject.

"There are so many of us, Jane, who went through the wars. So many who have come home with memories. And there were so many who didn't come home. I've been trying to figure out, not so much why I got to come home, as what it is that I'm supposed to do now that I'm here."

Not really understanding where this was leading, Jane offered only a quiet, "Is that what the book's about?" Hector didn't answer for the space of about five steps, then turned and looked at the girl beside him.

"Well, in a way. You're old enough so that if you were a boy you could have been drafted in time to go to Korea, but that's an experience you'll never have. I don't think you will have missed anything. But what this is about, this book of mine, is what those of us who did serve, who did experience the war, are going to do with what we learned."

They stopped now, by the railing of a small park near Jane's house. Hector turned to the girl, still holding her hand, and looked at her for a moment before going on.

"I don't mean the soldier skills. I mean what we learned about living, about fear, about missing something precious. That is what Second Lives is about."

The girl looked up at him, her eyes searching his to see if she could read more of the story there. Instead she found his eyes drawing her closer, just as he found hers drawing him to her.

The kiss was at first a light, almost brushing contact, but then it began to take on a force neither had expected. Their lips held for a long, breathless moment, before parting. Jane's stomach was giddy, and the effect on Hector was only slightly less. Their eyes held each other until Hector broke into a smile, and Jane giggled before taking a breath. In that few moments all of Jane's fears about her relationship with this man flew up into the night sky.

"Did Hector kiss you?" Sis asked with a smile in her voice. "I looked out the window and I thought that's what I saw."

Jane, her face a little flushed, looked at her roommate with a slightly bemused expression, and didn't answer. Instead she walked across the room to the same window and looked out. Hector was still at the railing, facing slightly away from the building, looking toward the river. As she watched, he turned, looked up at the dark window, waved almost too casually, and began walking away. She followed him with her eyes until he turned the corner and was gone.

Jane was not a dreamy school girl, so her answer was not a wide-eyed, breathless response. Instead she said rather slowly, as if considering exactly what had happened out there against the fence, "Yes, a kiss. I don't know if he meant it to happen. I don't know if I did. But it did. And it seemed alright." She looked at Sis and then, after a pause, said, "What do you think?"

"I think he's as much a mystery as ever," Sis responded.

Chapter 13 - Love Comes In

On the morning after Jane and Hector had their unexpected and thoroughly enjoyable first kiss, Hector rose as usual just after first light. The morning sun lit the long street, and the buildings and windows bounced it into his room. As the intensity of the light grew with the morning, Hector found himself sitting at his desk, his manuscript before him, a page or so of notes to remind himself of changes he wanted to make, but the hand that held the papers was stayed by the man's inner thoughts.

What had happened last night, in front of Jane's apartment, was still playing in his mind. The expression on his face was one of bemusement, as though he were watching a light, romantic comedy on the big screen at the Warner theater several blocks away. He smiled, he frowned, he stared off into space, he did not work.

Jane's sleep, though untroubled, was nevertheless not as restful as usual. Her dreams repeated the events of the night before, and her arms seemed to be hugging a large, firm pillow. When she awoke, that was exactly what she was doing, and it made her laugh. For a languorous half hour she remained in bed, alternately dozing and waking, Hector uppermost in her thoughts. Had last night been a dream then? No, she was perfectly aware of the change in her life, and her thoughts went from amazement at Hector's actions (as well as her own, she had to admit), to amusement, to serious evaluation of her own life.

Since high school, Jane had been a working girl. At first, like most of her classmates, she looked on work as simply an interim occupation until she found a man who would give her the home and family and future most young people, boys and girls, men and women grew up expecting. With her growth into an independent, and not very lonely young woman, she began to value the control she had over her own life. Despite the long hours, she really enjoyed her job, and wasn't looking for it to "lead somewhere," as so many of her classmates did. She enjoyed the interaction with strangers, with people she saw every day, and with the close community of the Vienna's family. By now, she realized, her parents had stopped asking about her plans, stopped intimating that she must be looking forward to something more than being a waitress.

The city of Washington was a magnet for young girls eager to strike out on their own and, at the same time, a potential graveyard for hopes and dreams of marriage, family and home. Since the days of World War I, the ratio of women to men had been decidedly in the men's favor. The surplus of singles, augmented each year by the latest influx of new civil servants, meant that the competition for attractive men was quite keen. It also meant an over-supply of office workers who became dedicated and effective in managing the daily business of government. They formed a kind of mid-level, powerful, administrative force, one that was at the same time hidden and un-named. For many of the young women, their personal lives soon revolved around their jobs. They lived in shared rental homes and apartments and in residential hotels like the Chaselton, on 16th

Street, where "house mothers" attempted to keep watch over the social lives and morals of their young residents. It was dormitory life on a more independent scale.

The young men who came to the city were often better educated, with professional jobs and aspirations. Many had come as Hector had, during war-time, and had stayed on to complete their education, or to move from military assignments to civilian jobs in the same service. Many entered professions that were outside the government, but still dependent on it. Their attractiveness to the young women made them objects to be obtained in a fierce competition that often led to disappointment and heartbreak. It was in this atmosphere that people like Hector, and like Jane, found themselves often on the social rim, rather than in its interior swirl. Neither met the physical criteria of the "first echelon" of the time, but neither were they unacceptable. They were average in looks, perhaps a little awkward on Hector's part, and a little plain in Jane's case, but still not excluded from social circles. Both, however, were unusual in that they were, at least on the surface, comfortable with their own lives, and with themselves.

It was in this atmosphere that Jane and Hector found themselves suddenly thinking beyond today, looking with some expectancy toward a future different from the present.

Hector approached the Vienna with an awareness unusual for him. Normally he would have left his room at the King of Rumania about 11:30, and walked almost automatically down the block to the corner, across the street to the other side, then up the block to the restaurant. Entering it, he would scarcely look around, heading directly to his table along the wall, seating himself, taking his notebook and pen from his pocket, and placing them on the table. Today, however, he was outside the restaurant before it opened for lunch, and walking back and forth several times, as much as half a block in either direction, before actually going inside. Today he stopped at the counter, looking around, before seeing Jane. Then, his eyes mostly on her, he walked to his table. She had seen him come, because she had been watching for him. She had noted his first pass by the door, and his second and even the third before resuming the business of setting up her tables. When he came in she began moving toward him, their paths joining at the table.

"Good morning, Jane." His voice was slightly strained in his greeting.

"Good morning, Hector," Jane countered. They looked at each other, smiled, then just stood for a second.

Hector began again: "G-good morning. A-about last night." Jane's heart did a curious sort of slow "thump pause thump" at the words.

"Hector, I—."

Her words were interrupted by his own: "What happened—," again a pause, while Jane's eyes focused on his face and felt moistness in her own, "I really meant it," Hector finally was able to say.

"Oh!" was all Jane could muster. Hector slowly sat and looked up, first in the mirror, that surface that had been their two-way communication medium for so long, then turned to look directly at her.

"I hope you did, too," he said and smiled at her.

"Oh!" the girl said again. "Oh! Yes, I did, Hector." The tan she had acquired in Florida didn't quite mask the rising flush she felt. For several seconds there was no further conversation, if what they had just had was indeed a conversation at all. Hector let out a withheld breath, looked down at the tablecloth, and obviously trying to reconnect with normalcy, patted his pocket for his notebook and pen. Neither were there.

Their days now began and ended in each other's company, for the day really didn't have meaning until Jane arrived at the restaurant, and Hector came in for lunch. Late night rides on the streetcar, slow walks to her door, lingering goodnights in the doorway, or in the vestibule if the weather was bad, defined the end. Everything else, the customers in the Vienna, the words on Hector's pages, often had to fight for space in their thoughts. Though the level of physical intimacy did not escalate rapidly, and their conversations were often silent, there was a strengthening and tightening of their bond. Jane and Hector were a couple, and for them there was now bright promise where once there had been only gray tomorrows.

Chapter 14 - Sis Understands

Sis, of course, was also dealing with promise: her relationship with her own casual friend, Dean. Over the weeks of the summer she had been in Washington, Dean had become a more constant companion, beginning with the concerts at the Watergate, and flowing on to occasional dinners at Luigi's, and once in a while a movie at one of the grand downtown theaters off Pennsylvania Avenue. What began as casual encounters had developed a regularity that Sis didn't mind at all. Most of the other single men she had met, usually other Civil Servants, were her age or only a bit older. Dean was a much more stable, steady, mature man. His sense of adventure had been tempered by his time in the army, and he urged Sis to do only the kinds of things she was comfortable with. Still, she sometimes wondered about the things some of the other girls in the office giggled about on Monday mornings, and hoped she did not appear too prim in their eyes.

There had been a few dates with boys her own age back home, but it took only a time or two of going to the local Miners Union hall or VFW dances to know that drinking whisky with beer chasers was not her idea of a good time, and certainly not a safe time. For two years after college she had taught history at her old high school, but the prospect of growing old in a mining town, with a coal-pigmented husband and a house crowded with growing children, had led her to Washington, and it seemed, to Dean. But where was that, she wondered? So far there had not been even casual hand-holding. What was she missing? What did Dean want? She decided that she must find out.

Before the girls went to sleep that night, Sis had tried, without much success, to discover from Jane exactly how "the kiss" (she thought of it in quotation marks) had happened. Jane, however, was unable to offer more than, "It just did. I don't know why."

Dean was on the phone talking to Jane, when Sis entered the apartment on Tuesday after work. It had been a particularly tiring day for her, and she had been looking forward to a long bath and maybe a glass of wine before even thinking about eating. Instead, Jane looked at her, smiled and handed the phone to her, saying, "It's Dean. For you."

The black hard rubber receiver was warm from Jane's hand, and held a faint aroma of the perfume the older girl usually wore. Placing the telephone to her own ear, Sis's thoughts went from disappointment at the prospect of delaying her bath, to eagerness to talk to this slow-speaking, slow acting man. "Hi, Sis," Dean said. His deep, drawling voice greeted her with warmth. Her own voice immediately grew warm and eager.

"Hello Dean. I just walked in the door." She hoped her voice didn't sound as tired as she felt.

"If this is a bad time, I could call back later." Dean's considerateness was, Sis realized, one of the things she admired about him.

"No, no. I'm fine."

"Well," the man began, "I wondered if you would like to go to a dance Friday night?"

Sis quickly did a mental inventory of her closet, looking for something to wear to a dance, as she absorbed Dean's question. "A dance?" she temporized. "What kind of dance?" There was a slight pause as Dean, uneasy about dancing in the first place, tried to frame the correct answer.

"The West Virginia Society dance at the Shoreham."

"Sounds like high society to me," Sis countered. "I'm not sure I'm prepared to 'come out' in Washington yet." Her voice held a lightness mixed with apprehension.

"Not 'high society', West Virginia Society. Since almost nobody in Washington comes from here, there are state societies that kind of help people make a social life," Dean explained. "It won't be fancy, just coats and ties and party dresses."

By now Sis had finished considering her wardrobe and decided that the one cocktail dress she owned, an emerald-green taffeta she could wear 'off the shoulder', would be fine. "Yes, I'd love to go," she said.

"I'll pick you up about seven," Dean said. "And you don't have to eat. There will be plenty of food there."

It was, in fact, a "get acquainted" dance that the society always held in September. Since the idea was to encourage new members, drawing from the large number of new government employees who came to the city after every high school and college graduation, the dance and the food were free—a fact Sis didn't appreciate until someone they talked to during the evening made a comment about it. Dean had laughed, letting Sis know that it was part of an open secret among those who had been in Washington for a long time: these dances were one of the places to find a free meal and entertainment, at least once a year. There were many such societies in the city, but the largest, perhaps because so many new government workers were recruited from the states they represented, were West Virginia, Pennsylvania and North Carolina. Virginia, maybe because the word "society" had a much more important meaning in that state, was never a very active one.

"It's not important that you come from West Virginia," Dean had explained, "only that you're here with someone who did." For Sis, the idea that people would find it necessary to seek out people "from home," was a curious one. Her excitement at leaving the small Allegheny valley and village was enough to sustain her during the first months in the city. Since then her problem had been not having enough time and opportunity to take advantage of all there was to do, rather than finding someone to do it with. Dean, in his reserved, almost shy way, had become a frequent accompanist as she learned the rhythms of the city. Tonight he had introduced her to just another measure of the community she had joined in the Spring.

"Dean's not a bad dancer," Sis found herself thinking, and then wondered why it surprised her. She enjoyed being held close by him, and swirling around on the large dance floor was exciting. Dean, for all his soft and slightly overweight appearance, had tonight presented himself at her door in a neatly pressed suit, a white shirt and a bow tie. The horizontal line of the tie went well, she thought, with the wide face and warm smile she had come to look forward to seeing. Holding her, leading her around the floor, he exhibited a quiet competence. It was, she thought, very comfortable here in his arms.

When, at midnight, the small band segued into *Good Night Ladies,* and the crowd began doing the things people do at the end of a party, Dean and Sis waltzed slowly to the old tune, and when it was over, stood quietly for a moment, looking at each other, before Dean broke the spell by saying, "Time to go, I guess. Have you enjoyed it?"

Sis, still in the spell of the last dance, gazed up at her escort before saying only, "Uh huh. Yes. Yes, Dean. Thank you very much." Her voice was subdued and smiling with an inner warmth.

"We don't have to take a cab, Dean," Sis said as they walked out of the hotel.

"It's late," Dean responded, but the young woman on his arm was in no hurry to end the evening. And in her mind was Jane's description of the streetcar ride and then the slow walk with Hector only a few weeks earlier. What would happen if she and Dean took a long ride and a slow walk tonight, she wondered.

"Can't we take a streetcar from here?"

"No, but we can walk up to Connecticut Avenue, and catch one there," Dean replied, "then transfer to the one going to your place when we get to K Street."

"Lovely," Sis said, and they began walking toward the avenue. Whether it was her act or his, the two found their hands interlocked as they walked along the broad sidewalk.

Chapter 15 - Looking Back

The weather was slowly cooling, the leaves turning and falling. Nights were chilly, and for a few weeks the essence of mothballs charged the air as sweaters and jackets came out of their summer closets. Not all buildings were air conditioned, and even in those that were, management held to a strict calendar when it came to turning off the cooling and turning on the heat. Hector wore his sweater most days now, and for the first time in years seemed to notice the changes in his surroundings.

On this particular day, some six weeks after Jane and Hector "discovered" each other, the morning sky was darker than usual. The wet streets no longer had the steamy odor of a summer shower, but instead an acrid and not quite fresh smell. On the broad sidewalks, populated by old trees, the wet leaves began to release their fall perfume. Tires made a swishing noise and often sent up flares of water that collided with the curbs and shot up onto stockings and pant legs. Getting off the streetcar, Jane opened her umbrella and made her way across the street to the Vienna's entrance. Shaking off the water, she went inside.

She began her day's work without giving much thought to what she was doing. The repetitive process she had followed for so long allowed her to think about other things. Most days now, her thoughts turned to Hector. Today, however, she let her mind drift in a slightly different direction.

Usually when Jane let Hector into her conscious mind, she thought about what he was like, what life with him might be, how he had brought something fulfilling to her life. Today she seemed focused on another part of Hector. A part they had not talked about too much since that night so many months ago, when he told her about his war.

Jane had awakened earlier than usual, and Sis, still getting ready to leave for her office, had started yet another conversation about Hector and his war record. Her brother, Sis thought, was being selfish and cold by not sharing the story with their parents. Try as she might, Sis reported, she could not get her brother to tell her, or the family, what he had done, what had happened to him. Jane quickly understood that her roommate was expecting her to help.

"Is it really important," Jane asked? "He doesn't talk to me about it."

Sis was silent while she finished dressing, but then, just as she was putting her raincoat on, she said: "Maybe you don't want him to be a hero."

"No," Jane said quickly. "It isn't that. It's just that's not what your brother and I talk about."

"Well, I wish you would. You have a lot more influence over him than I do."

Now, in the restaurant, Jane heard Sis's words again. Was she jealous of Jane's intimacy with her brother? Or was the younger girl simply frustrated that her own brother, the one hero of her childhood, was unwilling to let the world know how much of a hero he really was? As she moved around the tables Jane resolved to bring the subject up with Hector when he took her home after work.

"Hector," Jane began tentatively, "was the war really that bad?" They were walking hand-in-hand along the broad avenue near Jane's apartment. At the word "bad," Jane felt Hector's fingers tighten suddenly, then relax. Maybe she should not have asked the question. For a few paces the man said nothing. Then he began to reply, hesitantly at first, but then running his thoughts and words almost together.

"Yes. Well, not all of it, maybe. Sometimes, when the guns were quiet, when we weren't being attacked, it was—well, almost a good time. I mean," he paused, "I mean it was a time when you really appreciated your buddies, knew they were on your side, would fight for you and expected you to fight for them. That felt good." He paused. "See, Jane, in a place where you are being threatened every day, where you can't really relax, it's a great thing to know that you have friends who will be there for you, especially in a dangerous situation. It's something you can't imagine."

"I can't imagine any of it," Jane confessed. In a way she was sorry she had started the conversation. She could end it now, she thought, because Hector himself had stopped. If she said no more, maybe he would begin again, but if he didn't, she could leave it at that. Later she would regret not making that choice. Now she said, "Would you ever consider writing the story of what happened?" That might satisfy Sis, Jane thought.

Instead, Hector looked at her sharply, shook his head, and said, "It's over Jane. That was someone else."

"No, Hector," Jane heard herself saying, "It was you. It is part of who you are, isn't it? Won't it always be?"

They were in front of Jane's building. Hector turned to her and said, in a very even voice, but one she felt was full of emotion, "That was someone else, Jane. Not me. I'm just a guy who has a book about to be published, and it isn't a war story." With that, Hector gave Jane a quick kiss, turned and walked away into the night.

Jane entered the apartment but didn't turn on the light. Closing the door, she turned and went into the kitchen, where the small window gave her a view of the courtyard behind the old house and the backs of the houses around her own. The window slid up easily, and Jane stood there, breathing deeply of the cool night air. She didn't look at the houses or yards, but rather, she looked upward, over the rooftops, at the black night sky. The crisp fall air was clear, and the stars were little glimmers of a distant world. Almost as distant as the world Hector inhabited, she thought. And just as filled with the unknown. Deep in her heart, Jane began to mourn, saying goodbye to the life she and Hector had begun to plan. She knew, without a word being spoken, that she had trespassed on a place in her man's life that would not bear turning over or cultivating. Yet she did not really understand what she had done. Why was it wrong, she wondered, to want to know (and to want others to know) all about a person you loved. Loved. A word she had not yet used with Hector, but now she said it aloud in the darkness of the room: "Love. I love you, Hector," she said. The sprinkle of stars was suddenly multiplying as her eyes filled with tears.

A scuffing sound caused the young woman to turn from the window. In the pale light she saw Sis, in pajamas and slippers, coming into the room.

"Jane?" Sis was only able to see a silhouette against the window.

"Yes," the other answered, her voice slightly strained.

"What are you doing standing in the dark?"

"I'm sorry," Jane responded. "I didn't mean to wake you."

"What is it?" Sis persisted. In the near darkness the two women moved to the small table and sat down facing each other.

"It's Hector," Jane replied. "After what you said this morning, I decided to ask him about the war. I did when we were on the way here from the restaurant"

"What did you ask him?" Sis's voice was a mixture of curiosity and concern.

For a moment Jane said nothing. Then she described the conversation, adding only that she was afraid she might have pushed Hector too far. "He seemed to suddenly cut me off," she said. "I just don't know. He might not feel he wants to see me again. Oh, Sis," the girl said softly, "I don't know what this is all about. Not my part, and certainly not yours. I don't want to hurt Hector." She turned away from Sis and looked again out the window. Sis turned, too, stood and left the room.

Sis was gone from the apartment by the time Jane awoke the next morning. Her sleep had been anything but restful. In her dreams she saw herself alone and drifting, not heading in any particular direction. From time to time she would see Hector, his back to her, walking in the mist. Turning, she would see Sis, a bright light behind her, standing and looking at Jane and Hector. The dream had neither beginning nor end. Once she was awake Jane gave the dream little thought, but found instead, her mind focusing on what she wanted from Hector.

That she was drawn to him, liked him more than any man she had ever known before, was obvious. She had, in fact, come to that conclusion some weeks ago. But did she want him to marry her? Was she ready to commit herself to one person? She laughed at the idea that there were others in her life to choose from. If that was what she wanted, and what Hector wanted, she must find a way to repair what she knew was a breech in their relationship. But that was something she needed to understand more clearly before she could even talk to Hector about it.

Jane continued to examine what had happened the night before as she rode the swaying streetcar to K Street. It was a gloomy fall morning, and the windows were closed, trapping the dampness and body heat of the passengers in the air. The warmth was comforting, though the closeness made Jane's still weary mind less focused. When she arrived at the Vienna she was still unclear about where she and Hector stood. On one hand, she felt, Hector's past was his own. On the other, if she was to truly give herself to him, he must do the same with her. Otherwise—well, there was no otherwise, was there?

As he had on the morning after their first kiss, Hector made his way to the Vienna, but walked back and forth past the building before making up his mind to enter. He needed to talk to Jane, and he needed to do it face to face. Hector was not one to use the telephone except for the most brief exchanges. He needed to see his respondent when he talked; to see the expression on the other's face as ideas were exchanged, thoughts spoken aloud, words precisely placed in order. Where Jane was concerned, he could not even comfortably lift the phone and call her to say they needed to talk. After several slow passes at the door, he turned and entered.

From her usual place at the back of the room, Jane saw Hector come in. "Valery," she said to the hostess, "I need to talk to Hector."

"Go ahead, Honey," Valery said. "I know something's bothering you. We can handle your tables for you." Valery was not only a good employer, Jane knew, but a friend too. Taking off her apron, Jane met Hector before he crossed the room to his table. "Can we go outside and talk?" she asked. Hector, somewhat startled by Jane stopping him in the middle of the room, blinked, looked around at his table and then at Valery, then back to Jane. Without speaking, he turned and walked to the door. He held it open for the young woman, and they left the restaurant.

Sis sat at her green metal desk in the outer office. In her typewriter was a nearly completed analysis her chief needed for a two o'clock meeting. It was almost noon. She had been working on the report since nine o'clock, her mind constantly switching between her work and her very uncomfortable date with Dean the night before. He had taken her to dinner at Mama's, the Italian restaurant just south of Dupont Circle. Over cannelloni and manicotti, they talked quietly, as they usually did. On this night, however, the conversation seemed to focus on Hector. Sis had raised, again, the story of what was coming to be known as "Hector's War." It wasn't a subject Dean enjoyed discussing, but Sis did. Tonight she pursued it as if she thought Dean was hiding the full story from her. "Why won't you tell me what it was like for Hector?" she asked.

"Because I wasn't there, Sis, and I really don't know."

"Surely you talk about it," she said, sounding convinced of her own position.

"No," Dean responded. "Actually, it isn't something I want to know about in the first place, and in the second, if Hector wanted me to know, he would tell me." Sis was about to respond, when Dean went on: "Look, Sis, I know how much the story means to you, and that you want your dad to know, but this is something that only your brother can do. Or not do." Dean paused and looked directly into Sis's eyes. She blinked, then looked away.

"You don't understand," she said.

Reaching across the red and white checked tablecloth, Dean took her small hands in his, covering them completely, and still looking intently into her eyes, said, "Yes, I do understand, Sis, but I think I understand Hector, too. And that means that I know what his experience was like, even if I wasn't there, and I know that it is something intense and personal and not in the history books." Sis pulled her hands from his, put them in her lap, and turned away.

Instead of just saying, "Come in," Hector responded to the knock at his door by opening it. He was surprised to find Dean leaning casually against the door frame, a bemused smile illuminating his face. It was the sort of look he might have given a student in one of his government classes after he surprised him by calling on him for an answer. It was about ten in the morning, and Hector had been at his desk since just after sunrise, unproductively staring at the pages he was supposed to be revising. Dean's arrival was a welcome excuse to put the papers back in the box. Hector, his voice sounding as if he had been expecting his friend, said "Come in, Dean."

"You busy?" Dean asked.

"Not like I should be," Hector replied. "I'm having some trouble keeping my mind on my work, at the moment."

"I shouldn't wonder," Dean drawled. Hector liked Dean's slow cadenced speech—not really country, but richer and more colorful than most.

Dean looked around the room. He realized that the only chair was at Hector's desk. If they were both to sit, one would have to use the bed. Dean walked over and lowered himself gently onto the blanket. He noted that the cover was taut, the corners even and neatly folded. "Make your own bed, I see," this with a rumbling kind laugh.

"Well," Hector responded, "remake it. Conditioned by ten years of doing it that way, I guess."

Dean looked out the window, then at the desk and typewriter. Hector still stood near the door. He looked at his friend. His face gave no evidence of what he was thinking. If indeed he was thinking at all. Dean studied his friend's expression.

"Are you and Jane okay?"

Hector looked directly at Dean and said, "I don't know. We haven't stopped seeing each other, if that's what you mean. We just don't seem to be talking very much."

Again Dean looked at Hector's eyes. They were expressionless.

"I was married once," Dean said. "Did you know that?"

"No, I don't think so. What happened?"

"The easy answer is 'another guy,' I guess. But that's not really an answer."

Hector walked closer to his desk and looked out the window. He could see the Vienna, he realized, if he stood to one side and looked up the block. Funny, he thought, he'd never noticed that before. He said nothing, and Dean began to talk again.

"What really happened was that we stopped talking," the older man said. "We didn't know how, I guess, and so we just let things go." He stood up. "I think we kept hoping the other would start the conversation, or say what was wrong, or something, but we never did."

"Are you sorry?"

"I have regrets, Hector, because we might have worked it out, but all in all, I have come to think we weren't ready for marriage, either of us."

"Are you ready now?" Both were thinking about Sis.

"Maybe. But the next time will be different." Hector looked at Dean's face. He was smiling now. "What I have learned, Hector, is that if a person is important to you, then you have to be as ready to say the hard things as the easy ones. And you have to say them when it is fresh in your mind. You can't wait for the 'right moment,' or plan how you are going to say it. If it is hard, the words are never the right ones, but if you love each other, and you want to keep that love, you need to take the risk of talking about what is troubling you. You can't just walk away and hope it will resolve itself. Does that make sense?"

Hector watched the last line of the sun disappear below the Arlington skyline as he leaned once again on the iron railing at the edge of the Tidal Basin. The day had grown slightly colder as the sun left the sky. The air began to penetrate his sweater, a condition that seemed to return his thoughts to the present. He stood up and turned back to the city. It was time he returned to the Vienna, and to Jane.

Chapter 16 - Author, Author

When Hector became famous it was, like most things in his life, unintentional. He was a man who followed where life led, taking turnings as they came. He didn't seek, yet he became sought after. He became the voice of a new generation; a generation invented by events.

Jane and Hector had quietly married some six months earlier. His newly achieved celebrity had brought a measure of financial independence, and they had moved to a bright and large apartment overlooking Dupont Circle, near the Crystal. They often ate out, but seldom at the Vienna, though for neither of them was food as important as the presence of the other. Sometimes there were a few friends at the table, but not often. For two people who had been so independent of others, so comfortable being single and alone, their happiness in each other was palpable.

In the end it wasn't Doubleday, but another, smaller publisher geared more toward unknown writers, that brought out Second Lives. Still, the advertising budget was more than adequate, according to Margery Maxwell. And the resulting royalties were a pleasant surprise to the now successful writer.

Hector was seated in his usual chair at the Vienna, facing the mirror. Across the table a reporter from the Evening Star was listening with grave attention.

"I never thought about writing a book when I began Second Lives," Hector told the interviewer. "I was simply trying to understand my generation, what had happened to those of us who came of age in time to go to the war. The wars," he corrected himself. With his book showing signs of success the reluctant author found that he could easily provide satisfactory answers to questions he didn't necessarily understand. What he did understand was that the picture he had produced of his generation was considered by those who read it to be accurate and honest. But he was both amused and unsettled by the gravity given his pronouncements by reporters.

Though his parents and their contemporaries and those just entering adulthood were happy to be alive in a world at peace, and enjoying the prosperity it was bringing, Hector and some others in his generation wondered what they could do with what they had won. Hector thought that there should be something beyond winning, more than peace and personal pursuits. Would they all just become complacent, pliant citizens, at ease with the world as it was, even as they thought it had been in the past? Hector didn't think so. Not much given to original thinking, nor to philosophical rumination, Hector surprised himself with the thoughts that began developing in his mind.

There had never been a "calling," if indeed there was one now. Hector was not a man of action, despite his military biography. He was not a deep thinker. He was simply himself. He responded to events. He didn't make them happen. Now, as his success brought him into greater contact with the world around him, he felt exposed and somewhat uncomfortable. He was, in fact, terrified of the unreal, surreal world his growing fame had opened before him. Still he could not ignore the call inside his head, any more than he had been able to on that dark night on the

Korean hillside. His weapon of choice now, however, was words. He picked them up as he needed them, hurling them, rolling them, leaving them to be ignited by readers and interviewers. His target now was not a three-dimensional enemy, but a ghostly presence. He sensed, rather than saw, a world in which there were people who had been affected by the decades of war, of license, of ruin, of war again. They wanted something better. The technology of war had made the world less remote and separated. People everywhere knew now that there were other places, other ways, and they were beginning to demand change. Hector's characters wanted to be the agents of that change.

Hector still used the Vienna as a place to meet reporters and other professional contacts, and on occasion, people whose society he was unsure about encouraging. Today he was sitting at his usual table, talking quietly with Ernest Holloway. Ernest was a tall, blond man of about forty. His clothes were business-like, and he presented himself with a professional air. Ernest represented a veteran's group with the lofty name of "Warriors at Peace." It was a loose collection of veterans, most of whom it turned out, had not seen their war as intimately as had Hector. In fact he was hard pressed to discover any combat veterans in the governing body of the organization.

"What we are trying to do is establish a voice," Holloway was saying. "So that next time our leaders begin to talk about saving the world, they will have someone to listen to who might disagree with them. Right now, for instance, in Indo-China, there are people fighting for the freedom of their own country, and the French are trying their best to stop them. What would happen if they asked us, again, to help them out?" Hector didn't know. The other man went on: "Our politicians seem to think that—" Hector lost interest in what his companion was saying almost as soon as the word "politician" entered his consciousness. In the months since the book had come out, Hector had become aware of certain words and phrases that were increasingly used in conversation. "Politician" was one. So was "Freedom loving," and the one that grated on him most, "the people."

Talking to Jane about it later that day, Hector realized that there was something wrong with what he was hearing. "The guy I had lunch with today, the one from the Warriors at Peace, kept talking about 'the politicians' and 'the people' and 'peace with our enemies,'" Hector said, emphasizing the phrases.

"What did he want from you," Jane asked?

"I think," Hector replied, "that he wanted my name."

"Your name?"

"Uh huh. To make people think I agree with what the organization stands for."

"Do you," Jane asked?

"Hard to say," her husband replied. "I'm not really sure what that is. What the organization stands for, or what these people expect from me." In fact, Hector realized, he wasn't even sure why he was allowing so many new people into his life at all. Certainly Margery encouraged him to give interviews because the publicity helped with the book sales, and that translated into even more money, but there was, in Hector's mind, a limit to that too.

"If you could do anything you wanted," Jane asked, "what would it be now?"

"I don't know. I don't know if I want to write another book, at least right now. I just want to live quietly, with you. I really don't like being out in public, being quoted, interviewed, made up to. I'm not at home with all this fame." Hector looked at Jane. She was sitting beside him on the comfortable sofa that had been their second purchase. Hector's desk was the first. The sofa was a very comfortable, thickly upholstered piece, a neutral gray.

The living room was painted a stark white, the hardwood floors were light oak. Windows faced Connecticut Avenue. They were long, almost reaching the floor, and the room had a ceiling ten feet high. The room overlooked the avenue just where the streetcars went underground. Hector found the muffled noise of the cars a restful and reassuring sound.

Getting up, he walked to the window. Turning to Jane, he asked: "What about you? What do you want now?"

Jane looked at him, then altered her gaze slightly to look out the uncurtained window. "You know, I really liked working. Liked meeting people, liked being in the middle of something outside myself." Her tone was thoughtful. "I know I don't need to work, and you might not like it if I went back to the Vienna, but I think I need to do something." As with anything Jane had to say, this was not presented with any urgency, but rather with a characteristically quiet assertion. The words fell softly on Hector, allowing him to absorb them without reacting. The silence that followed was not empty. Hector and Jane looked at each other, and then he walked over to where she was now standing, put his arms around her, and gave her a gentle, long hug. They kissed in that slow, provocative way they had evolved, and still clinging to each other, walked into the other room.

Much later, walking back from dinner at the little restaurant across the avenue, Hector held Jane's hand in his, and they walked at an easy pace.

"What I'd like to write about," he began, "is how the older people, my age, say, and even those who are just in their twenties, fit in jobs that people usually get right out of school."

Jane looked up at him. "Isn't that what you've already written about?"

"Not really. Second Lives is about going to school long after you should have, and finding yourself learning about things you might have been part of, or things you had heard of a long time ago, but now are hearing about them as if they were new. You know," he said as they reached the door to their building, "there are men and women of 21 or 25 or 30, who served all during the years they might otherwise have been apprenticing, or starting at the bottom in some job that would lead to a career. Now, if they are graduating from college or even high school after their war service, they're competing with new kids five or even ten years younger."

Reaching their apartment door, Hector fished the key from his pocket. Putting it in the lock, he swung the door open and stepped aside for Jane to enter. Once the door closed, he continued. "They are competing with 17- and 18-year-olds. That must be hard." Hanging up their coats, Hector followed Jane into the big kitchen.

"Should I make some coffee," Jane asked? Hector nodded and took a seat at the white porcelain-topped table where they ate breakfast.

"I think," he continued, "that just because we served, we can't expect the rest of the world to readjust everything for us. We have made our contribution, we've been rewarded if we chose to take advantage of it, and we should move on." He was speaking quietly, not really directing his thoughts at Jane as much as at himself. He was following a line of thought that had started with the questions Jane had asked earlier, but he was now testing the words he spoke by listening to them, feeling his way through new ideas.

Jane, for her part, was also thinking about their earlier conversation, listening to Hector with only part of her consciousness. She was considering the idea of being back at the Vienna, or maybe another restaurant, or even another kind of job. No, she really liked working in the Vienna, and felt so at home with the people and the routine. Yes, if she did what she wanted to do, she would try to get her old job back. Pouring out coffee for them both, Jane paused with the pot just above her own cup, turned to Hector, who was watching her.

"I think you've started another book."

He smiled and looked up at her.

"Yes, I think I have an idea. I need to talk to Margery in the morning."

"Hector," Jane said, putting the pot down on the stove, "I'm going to see if I can go back to the Vienna."

Chapter 17 - Sis and Dean

When Jane and Hector had married, Sis stayed on in the apartment. It suited her in size, convenience, and, most especially, in privacy. At Jane's request the landlord, whom Sis had never met, agreed to let her assume the apartment lease, and at the same reasonable rent. After two years in Washington, two years of being a "G-girl," Sis had settled into the life that called out to her. Satisfied at the moment with her job, Sis was enjoying life in the city.

April had given way to May, and the early heat of the season brought out the new spring wardrobes. The lighter-weight clothing matched the breezy and mild weather. The air held the smells of new growth and warm concrete, a mixture that, on a spring night, could be intoxicating to the romantic and eager couples who strolled the city streets.

Dean, nearing the end of his graduate studies, had gone from an internship to a part-time job in the office of one of West Virginia's congressmen. It wasn't an election year but that hardly mattered to his boss. Every day was part of an unending campaign to assure reelection, and Dean found himself working late night after night when the congressman was in the city. The apartment in Southwest was close to the House office building, and often Dean would knock at Sis's door late in the evening.

It was after nine when Sis looked down from her window and saw Dean at the front door. Smiling to herself, she ran down the stairs and opened it. Dean, his sparse hair more windblown than usual, his suit more rumpled than even he was comfortable with, followed the young girl up the stairs. Even without looking back Sis could feel his tiredness as he came up the steps.

In the apartment, Sis turned and Dean took her in his arms and kissed her gently, then more eagerly, as he felt the tiredness melt away. "Can you stay?" Sis asked.

"Of course," he replied.

"Have you eaten?"

"Lunch, I think," he said.

"Come into the kitchen."

While Sis made him a sandwich, they shared a beer and talked quietly. They asked about each other's day, they commented on whom they had seen or talked too, much like married couples do. But they were not married, nor had the subject ever come up. Sis wasn't any more eager for that than Dean at this point. As he ate, Sis looked at this man in her life, and felt the warmth he always brought out in her. She knew he was her man, and she was his woman, and that was as far as it went.

When Dean had pushed away the empty plate, they stood and walked back to the living room.

Again Sis asked, "Will you stay?"

And again Dean said "yes," whispering it in her ear.

"Are you very tired?" she asked.
"Not that tired," the man answered.

Dean was still asleep when Sis left for her office. She had set the alarm to give him time to go to his own apartment, dress and make a ten o'clock meeting on "The Hill." Though Dean didn't stay every night, they had evolved a certain routine, providing a certain amount of discrete cover for their relationship. Not that there were neighbors in the building who knew or cared, nor were there people in the surrounding houses to worry about. Still, what went on in private was best guarded, they agreed.

Sis had learned a good bit about privacy, and its importance since she had come to Washington. The strain caused by her probing of Hector's past, the wedge it had nearly driven between her and Dean, and between her brother and her sister-in-law, had taught her a lot. Hector, now successful and sought after, continued to protect his privacy, and Sis no longer was offended. Jane had been able to overcome Hector's defensiveness, and the subject of his war was never mentioned again. Yes, Sis had tried to tell their father about what she knew, but as he had always done, the man pushed the story aside and never asked about it again. At first Sis was crushed by the old man's response, but soon she allowed her thoughts to move away from the rejection and focus on simply being her brother's sister.

It was enough, she realized, that her brother was home and healthy, that he had found a life he was comfortable in, and that she and Jane could be friends.

Chapter 18 - Fame and Misfortune

*T**hey were a new generation—a generation of men and women who had in truth, been invented by events. "* So began the first page of Second Lives. *"They were born first as the generation of the end of the Jazz age and the beginning of the Depression. They had grown to adolescence and some even to adulthood by the time the war began, and certainly by the time it had ended in Korea. A period spanning little more than a decade, from 1941 to 1953, and then they were reborn. They were a new people when they returned from the wars, and they didn't quite know how to define or identify themselves."* Hector did that for them.

Second Lives told of their abrupt rebirth as a new people, conceived in service to a great cause. Not all were solders, of course. Many, especially women, were "war workers," holding jobs vital to sustaining the war effort.

"All had this in common:" he wrote, *"they were not the people their parents had been, or the people their parents expected them to be. They were of a new world. A world their*

younger siblings and their parents did not always understand. Newly born, they came with a past and a future, and a lot of catching up to do."

It was of them that Hector had written, and it was for them that the book had the most meaning. There were other books by other writers, of course. Books that would last longer, be more appreciated by a larger audience, but that was because they wrote of their war. Hector wrote about their new lives, and they outgrew them, and they moved on. Hector did not. In time he was reduced to being a spokesman for a generation that no longer had a need to be heard.

At first, work on the new book was interrupted by requests for articles and essays from Red Book, Liberty, the VFW magazine and others. Hector became adept at stating in new ways the same thesis he had offered in the book. As the interest in what he had to say declined, he was able to spend more of his time working on the outline of the work he had started referring to as "the sequel." He thought he had a pretty clear idea of what he wanted to say, and even found some characters to say it for him.

Chief among them was Homer Carlsen, a man of about thirty-seven, married, father of two small children, working as a salesman in one of the new post-war industries. Homer traveled for his company, working out of the main office in a suburb of Pittsburgh. On the road six days a week, he encountered many of his own kind struggling, as he was, to adjust their own lives to the places available to them.

If there was to be an antagonist, Hector felt, it would have to be modeled on Ernest Holloway, of the *Warriors at Peace* organization. Holloway had finally given up trying to recruit Hector, but he remained a focus of concern in the writer's mind. By putting him into Homer's story, Hector thought that he might finally be able to understand what the man really wanted.

Hector sat at his desk, comfortable with the heavy, modern shape of the light oak. The chair he used was also oak, but much darker and of an older style. He and Jane had found it one Saturday among other used furniture in a small shop in Mount Pleasant. A good cleaning had brought out the natural beauty of the wood. It was a swivel chair, just like the kind he had used in the army. When he worked, he sat straight, elbows barely touching the arms of the chair.

It was June, about the middle of the month, when the letter arrived. Hector was going through the day's mail when he came to it. It was a subpoena, calling Hector to a hearing by a Congressional sub-committee that was charged with investigating the spread of Communism. As he read the letter he pushed the chair away from the table. His erect posture seemed to melt slowly into a slump. He thought he knew what the committee and its investigators were looking for. Everyone in Washington understood that. They were trying to root out threats posed by something called the "international Communist conspiracy." But how Hector fit into that scheme, he did not understand.

In all the discussions and newspaper articles he had seen and heard, nothing demanded his attention or allegiance. Nothing except a report that he had heard on a radio newscast, that the *Warriors at Peace* leadership was being investigated. His lack of curiosity was not a conscious act, Hector knew. He simply didn't have the kind of mind that pursued details unless they were related to something that directly concerned him. So when the subpoena arrived, Hector was surprised, but only mildly curious.

"Did you get a lot done today," Jane asked. Most evenings, when Jane wasn't working, they would sit near the window overlooking the avenue, and talk about the day. Sometimes, but not always, they would have a glass of wine, or share a beer, which they sipped as they talked.

"Um, yes. Well, no as a matter of fact," Hector said. "I was writing pretty well most of the morning, until the mail arrived."

Reaching for the envelope that was on the bleached oak coffee table in front of the sofa, Hector handed it to Jane.

Jane looked at the paper without reading it. Handing it back, she asked: "What's this?"

"It says I have to come before the Robinson Commission in the House of Representatives."

"The what?" Jane's question was marked by only a little more curiosity than Hector's.

"The Robinson Commission" he replied. "That House committee that Dean is working for."

"I hear people talking about it sometimes at the Vienna," Jane said, nodding. "Sounds scary. What do they want to talk to you about?"

"I don't know. I haven't paid that much attention to what they are all about." It was a position, Hector would soon discover, that wasn't very wise or comfortable.

"Sis," Hector said when she answered the phone, "is Dean with you?" Hector knew that unless the man was at his Capitol Hill office, Dean could almost always be found at Sis's, regardless of the hour. It was eight o'clock on the evening the letter had arrived.

"No, Hector, he hasn't come home yet." Sis's response, that Dean "hasn't come home yet," hardly registered in her brother's mind. Standing by the desk, Hector shifted his weight from one foot to the other, turning slightly to look at Jane.

"I need to talk to him, Sis," Hector said.

"Call him at his office, I'm sure he's still there."

"Umm, I don't want to do that, Sis. But will you have him call me when he gets in?"

"Sure," the girl replied. "Is something wrong, Hector? You sound a little tense."

"I don't know, Sis. Just ask Dean to call, okay?"

Chapter 19 - Hector and Dean

It was nearly ten o'clock when the phone beside the sofa rang. Jane, after a day at the Vienna, had gone to bed. Hector, sitting at his typewriter, thinking about his story but not writing, responded slowly to the insistent bell. He walked across the large living room, and picked up the receiver on the seventh ring. "Hello," he said in his quiet voice.

"Hi, 'H'," Dean said, using the single letter Hector had become known by at the Crystal. "Sis said you wanted to talk to me. I guess I know what it's about."

"Do you?" Hector responded. His voice was casual, not cool. Picking up the envelope, he shook the subpoena out onto the coffee table. "What's going on, Dean?"

There was a short period of silence before Dean cleared his throat and drawled, "Well, the committee got hold of records from *Warriors at Peace*, and I found your name on Holloway's appointment calendar."

"That was a long time ago," Hector replied. Hector raised his head, turning toward the window overlooking the street, almost as if he were trying to see across the city into Sis's apartment. "I haven't talked to him in more than six months."

"There were also a couple of letters, offering you a place on their board."

Hector regarded the file drawer of his desk, and then the waste basket, before answering. "Maybe. But I just throw that kind of stuff away, man."

It was Dean's turn to say, "Maybe."

"What the hell do you mean, Dean? Maybe! I stopped talking to Holloway when he started telling me about what he called 'the politicians.' I have no time for them." Though his voice was calm, his face was becoming more red.

"Don't tell me, Hector. Tell the committee. Look, officially I'm not even talking to you, understand? Just report when you're told to and answer the questions you're asked." Dean's voice grew distant and cold.

Holding the receiver away from his ear, Hector looked at it, as if Dean's face might appear there. Bringing the phone back to his ear, he said simply, almost coldly, "Thanks for the advice, Dean." Both receivers clicked off at the same time.

He walked to the big window. He could look to the southwest and see the Capitol dome. Sticking his head out the window and looking straight south he could see the trees that marked Lafayette Park, and beyond that the lights of the White House. A little farther beyond the window ledge, and he could see the lights of the great mall where the memorials to Washington and Jefferson and Lincoln defined that part of the city. He stood still, at ease, yet at the same time more tense than usual. He stared out into the night.

Jane's hand pressed lightly on his shoulder. He looked at her face, saw the eyes looking up at him, and the lips that always spoke his name in a special way. Turning, he took her in his arms.

Later, as they were relaxing into sleep, Jane pressed closer to her husband and said, "I know it will be okay, Hector. It will."

Hector was up before Jane the next morning. When she came to the table for breakfast she saw that Hector was again looking worried.

"Are you thinking about the Committee?"

"Sort of. I'm really thinking about Dean. I don't guess he owes me anything, but I almost got the feeling he and the others on the committee had already made up their minds about me and that damned organization."

He poured Jane's coffee into the delicate china cup he had bought for her in one of the antique shops along the avenue. As he poured, he repeated nearly verbatim the conversation with Dean the night before. Jane listened, and agreed that it didn't sound like the Dean they both knew: easy-going, friendly, warm, protective. Had something happened between the two men that Jane didn't know about?

"No," Hector assured his wife, "unless he thinks I'm concerned about Sis." There seemed to be no conclusion they could draw, before Jane had to leave for the Vienna.

"I have to appear tomorrow afternoon," Hector said as Jane opened the door to leave.

"I know," she said. "I'll take tomorrow off and go with you." She closed the door and went down the stairs to the street. Hector, at the window, saw her step up onto the sidewalk from the entrance. When she had crossed to the streetcar platform, she looked back and up. They waved as the streetcar doors opened. Jane looked back once more as she stepped aboard.

The hearing was in a large conference room down a long marble corridor in the House Office Building. Hector and Jane walked slowly, hand in hand, looking for the room number. A guard at a cross-corridor pointed them in the right direction.

As they turned the corner to the right, several men, two with press cameras, looked up. They were standing near the door of the conference room. One of the reporters recognized Hector, and told his photographer to "get 'em." The camera came up, the flash went off and Hector and Jane, blinking from the explosion of light, stopped in front of the door.

"You coming to do research for your next book, Mr. Collin?" the reporter asked. "This your secretary?"

Smiling, Hector paused. "This is Mrs. Collin, Pete," Hector said.

"Oh! So you're here 'at the invitation of the committee' I guess," he observed.

At that moment the door opened, and Dean took Hector's arm, pulling him into the room. Jane was stopped abruptly by the closing door. Just before it closed, Dean gave Jane a slight smile and said, "I'll get him back to you soon." To Pete and the others, he said, "Sorry boys. You can have him when we're through with him."

Hector had turned quickly as the door closed behind him. He wanted Jane there, but had to settle for a brief look at her face, and the startled look she wore as Dean turned him toward the committee table.

Jane, taken aback by Dean denying her entrance, stood mutely in front of the door. From behind her, Pete said, "What's he being called for, Mrs. Collin?" Jane turned to the men before her.

"I—we—really don't know. Dean—Mr. Donovan—didn't say."

"You know him, then?"

"They were in school together." Jane stopped before talking about Dean and Sis, realizing that it was none of the reporter's business.

"Your husband certainly knows about us veterans," one of the other reporters said. The men nodded in agreement.

"Maybe he knows something about the people in the *Warriors at Peace* movement," Pete said.

"I don't know," Jane responded with a smile. She knew enough about people to recognize a friendly face when she saw it, and her instincts told her that Pete and his colleagues were, at least at this point, anxious to keep Hector a subject of admiration.

One of the men found a chair in a nearby cloakroom and brought it out.

"You might as well sit, Mrs. Collin. He's likely to be a long time."

The room was painted a dull cream color, with dark oak window frames, and an oak wainscoting that reached from the floor as high as the sills of the tall windows. The floor was uncarpeted, except for a rectangle occupied by the long table, with chairs for the committee on one side, and a single chair for Hector on the other. Dean sat at one end of the table.

Opposite Hector, in the center of the four men he faced, sat a young man with a thin face and a square jaw. Deeply tanned, his wavy dark brown hair was parted to one side. As he lowered his head a thick lock would fall across his face. With his hand he would push it back into place as he looked up, combing it with his fingers. His voice was harsh, nasal, distinctly New England.

"What is your relationship to the *Warriors at Peace*, Mr. Collin?" The tone of voice was of a man holding himself in check. Hector wondered at the interrogator's aggressive opening.

Before he could answer, another member of the committee asked, "Do you have counsel with you, Mr. Collin?" Hector looked at the other man. His accent neutral, perhaps southern or western, the man was older, a little heavier, somewhat balding.

"A lawyer?" Hector asked. "Why no. Why would I need a lawyer?"

The man spoke again, saying, "I hope you won't, Mr. Collin. I hope you won't." Hector looked at Dean. Dean looked down at the papers before him on the table.

"You were in Korea," Mr. Collin, the nasal voice began again. "Anything happen to you there?" The words were harsh on Hector's ear. The man held up what looked to be a copy of a military report, which he then passed to the man next to him.

"Is that my military record?"

"Answer the question, please," the sharp faced man responded.

"If that's my record, then you know what it says," Hector replied.

"I'm asking you," the lawyer said again. The trace of impatience in his voice was growing. Hector was trying to remain calm, but every word from the chairman's mouth pushed him backward toward that time so long ago. He placed his hands on the carved ends of the arms of the chair. Sitting straight, he brought his chin down, as if he were again on the parade ground.

"Sir." Hector began, reverting back to the respectful tone and slow cadence an experienced sergeant reserved for speaking to a junior officer. "With all due respect, I cannot see why my military record is being reviewed in this hearing. First of all, you have it in front of you, and whatever it says, I am sure it is correct. Second. ."

At this point the Boston lawyer jumped in abruptly: "Mr. Collin, I asked the question, and I expect an answer. I decide what questions get asked, and you, sir, are under obligation to answer them!"

The chairman, Hector realized, was responding just as a junior lieutenant would. It gave him some satisfaction to see that the game still worked. "Every solider who survives basic training," Hector thought to himself, "learns how to play with career-conscious second lieutenants." After ten years in the army, any soldier worth his rank could keep untested officers off balance. It seemed to work with lawyers, too, he noted with satisfaction.

"Sir," Hector began again, "I was sent to Korea as company sergeant. I served with a rifle company until I was wounded. I did what I was sent to Korea to do, and I did it to the best of my ability."

The lawyer stared at Hector for a few seconds. Hector kept his eyes locked on the other man's, until the chairman looked away. Hector continued to keep his eyes focused on the man across the table. Inside, he was conscious of a grinding, enervating grip on his gut. He heard Dean shuffle papers, and out of the corner of his eye saw the other members of the committee turn to look at the chairman.

The man paused over the papers in front of him, seemed to study them with great concentration, before looking up at, and then past Hector. As if soliciting agreement from his committee, he looked down the table at the other members, then at Dean, before turning back to his papers. "We'll get back to that later. Now, Mr. Collin," drawing a deep breath, "just when did you first contact the *Warriors at Peace* organization?"

Staring at his questioner, Hector appeared to be gathering his thoughts. After what he felt was a suitable length of time, he looked at each of the men sitting across from him before returning his gaze to the chairman.

"Sir," again the quiet, enlisted-to-officer tone of voice, "I never contacted that organization." 'Give the answer to the question you are asked' was part of the old formula. Then say nothing more.

"I believe that is not correct, Mr. Collin."

"I never contacted that organization," Hector repeated.

Picking up a sheaf of papers beside him, the chairman thrust them toward Hector. Giving them a shake, he said, "Here are letters to you from Mr. Holloway, Mr. Collin. Do you deny receiving them?"

"No."

"Yet you deny having contacted the organization?"

"Yes."

"I don't think I understand, Mr. Collin." The tone was now saccharine, sarcastic. "If you received the letters addressed to you, how can you deny contacting the organization?"

"They contacted me, Mr. Chairman," Hector answered. He was tiring of the game he had initiated. "I did not reply to them, nor did I have any interest in them. Their chairman called me and asked for a meeting. We met for lunch in a restaurant. I told him I had no interest in what he was trying to do."

Still not satisfied, the chairman pressed ahead: "And just what were they trying to do, Mr. Collin?"

"I'm not really sure, Mr. Chairman. I just wasn't interested in whatever it was."

"Now, let me see if I understand this, Mr. Collin." The nasal whine of the voice barely concealed the speaker's disbelief. "You had lunch with a man who sent you letters you didn't answer, to talk about something you didn't understand, and on the basis of that one meeting you decided you weren't interested in what he had to say, so you never replied to his letters. Is that what this committee is supposed to believe?"

Hector looked at the men at the table, as if he were trying to judge the depth of their belief or lack of it. Concentrating on Dean for a few seconds, before looking back to the chairman, he sighed, then began again.

"Sir, if you are implying that I am not telling the truth, then that is what you probably believe. If you are asking me to confirm or deny that I am a part of the *Warriors at Peace* organization, then I can only repeat what I have said earlier: I do not have any clear understanding of what that organization is about, and I have never been a part of it. Whatever they want, whatever they do, I have to assume it has to do with veterans."

The man beside the chairman, who had been silent since his first question, interrupted, saying, "But don't you speak for the veterans, Mr. Collin?"

"I write about the people who are veterans, sir, but not about Veterans as such," Hector responded quietly.

"And what is the difference?" the questioner asked.

Hector paused and thought about the answer before replying: "I write about people who had put their own lives aside for a few years and how they have gone about starting over. What they have done since they were in the wars. That's all."

Before that line of questioning could continue, the chairman jumped back in. "I don't think you are being candid with this committee, Mr. Collin. But we will get to what we are after before we are through."

Sensing an interruption from his colleague, the lawyer concluded abruptly: "we will adjourn for now and ask—direct that you be here tomorrow afternoon at the same time." With that he banged his gavel sharply on the table, stood up and walked out of the room. His colleagues, including Dean, followed.

Dean stopped only briefly to say to Hector, "It doesn't help to get the chairman riled, you know."

Hector, bewildered at the turn the afternoon had taken, stood slowly and watched the others leave the room. The uniformed guard, who had remained in shadow throughout the hearing, stood up and stepped toward the door.

"This way, Mr. Collin." His voice was firm but quiet. "I wouldn't say anything to the press just yet, if I were you."

Hector stepped into the dim corridor to find Jane and the newsmen still there. Jane stood, smiling, as Hector came into the hall. Immediately the reporters were around him.

"Did you satisfy the committee, Mr. Collin?" one asked.

"Will you have a statement for the late edition," asked another. Hector raised his hand, to halt the questions.

"I don't know, boys. I'm still not sure I know what the committee wants to know."

"Will you be back?" asked the one who had first recognized him.

"Tomorrow," Hector said, and taking Jane's arm, the couple walked quickly away.

Chapter 20 - The Fall

When the committee had finished with Hector, he was indeed finished. After the second day of being questioned by the chairman, with little assistance from either his colleagues or from Dean, the writer was dismissed. As the members of the committee left the room Dean walked up to his friend and repeated the security guard's advice of the day before.

"I wouldn't give the press much time, Hector. They might blow this out of proportion."

"How much more proportion can it have?" Hector responded. "For the better part of two days I have sat here and been asked questions I couldn't answer, by a man who didn't listen, and now I'm 'dismissed.' I still don't know what he wants from me, and I don't understand what this committee is trying to do. It seems to me, Dean," his normally calm voice rising slightly in both pitch and volume, "people, even politicians, ought to know what they want before they go looking for it." With that, Hector turned from Dean and walked out through the open door, into the corridor.

"Mr. Collin!" It was the reporter from the Evening Star. "Mr. Collin, it sounds as if you were just a little hot there, just now." The guard had been holding the door open, and Hector realized that his remarks to Dean had been overheard. Hector stopped, looked briefly at Jane, who had waited again outside the door during the afternoon questioning.

Turning to the reporter, and then looking at the others grouped around him, Hector paused.

"I apologize if it sounded that way. I guess I am just a little upset about wasting my time listening to a man ask questions he either didn't expect an answer to, or using his time, and mine, and the time of everybody else in that room just to create a record for himself."

"What kind of record?" one of the other reporters asked.

"Well, I had a lot of time to think about what was going on in there, and frankly, it just felt to me that the man doing the questioning was trying to establish himself as a tough guy in the anti-Communist business."

"Why would he do that?" another asked.

"Maybe he wants to get elected to the Senate," Hector responded after a second or two. "Maybe he sees this as a way of separating himself from all the others he might run against."

The reporters scribbled for a few seconds before the Daily News man took up the thread. "You think there isn't anything to what these committees are looking for?"

"Well, I wouldn't say that there aren't some people in this country who follow the Communist ideas, and even some who support them. But first of all, I don't think it is much of a threat to our country. But you know," his voice was quieter now, "you know, we fought a war, well several wars, so that people could believe what they want. What really matters is that the majority of us believe the same thing, or nearly the same thing. That the way we live, the things we believe in, reflect what a whole lot of the world wishes it could have. And we're

117

not going to let that slip away. And we're not going to give it away to a few people who want to make their political lives by insisting that the freedoms we enjoy are a threat, and should be controlled." Taking Jane's arm, Hector left the reporters writing furiously, and quickly walked away.

The phone in the apartment had started ringing almost as the couple walked in the door. After the first few, all from reporters, Hector and Jane went out again, to spend a quiet couple of hours in a small restaurant around the corner. In the dimly lit dining room they blended into the scene, and Hector had time to catch his breath. Reaching across the table, Jane put her hand over his.

"Hector, what's going to happen now?" He looked up and into her eyes.

"I really don't know. I guess I should have followed Dean's advice and just said something like 'no comment.' But Jane, I was so angry by the time the day was over, I just lost control. I mean, what do these people expect? If I were a subversive agent, I certainly wouldn't tell them I was. I don't think they had anything they wanted out of me, and I certainly didn't need them to provide me with a platform. I just sort of let myself go."

Jane studied Hector for a few moments, then said, "Is this all about your honor, Hector? Is that what you're worried about? Is that why this matters so much?"

Hector considered the question. "My honor? Of course it is, Jane. Honor, and not forgetting the ones who didn't come home. Remembering why we, all of us, were fighting a war." He looked away, his eyes narrowing as he remembered a night in another life.

"It's my honor, yes. My commitment to them. That's why it matters."

"Will it be okay, do you think?"

Hector looked at Jane, then around the room. His gaze fixed on the big window, half obscured by sheer drapery. He could see people walking by outside, but only as vague shapes and shadows. "It all depends on those people out there, Jane. On how they see me, and how afraid they might have become after reading the newspaper stories about what people are saying in these hearings. My god, Jane, I hope I'm not going to become some sort of hero to the people who have been demonstrating against these committees." He looked back at his wife, drinking in her open, fresh looks, worried about the concern her eyes could not hide.

The phone began ringing early the next morning, and Hector found himself agitated and annoyed by it. His usual pattern, working quietly at his desk from the time Jane left for the Vienna until her return, often late in the evening, was fractured and disturbed. He thoughts wouldn't come, his mind wouldn't focus, and his ideas shot randomly around in his head. Finally, about noon, he picked up his notebook, now a leather, full-sized brief-case like affair, given him by Jane, made sure he had his pen and that it was fully charged with ink, and left the apartment.

Hector walked for nearly an hour, slowly progressing uptown, along Massachusetts Avenue. Near the Turkish Embassy he changed course, crossing over to Que Street, and then heading west into Georgetown. As he walked his thoughts calmed down, and he began to see the words he needed to write. As he walked past the library on R Street, he paused, then went into the building. It was early afternoon, and most of the tables in the main room were empty. Selecting one, he sat down, opened his notebook, and took out his pen. As the warm room enclosed him, his nostrils filled with the unmistakable odor of ink and paper and hard bindings, and he began to feel very much at ease. The words began to flow, his pen moving quickly and quietly across the page. For the next three hours he returned to his own world, cutting off the stressful and demanding real world he had created just the day before. He was again at peace. The change of place had been worth the walk.

Chapter 21 - Dean Recovers

The weather was turning again to Fall when Dean called Hector and suggested that they meet. Although Sis had called several times, and she and Jane had spent an occasional afternoon together, the two men had not spoken since the end of the hearing, several months before. Dean initiated the meeting.

"We need to meet, Hector," had been his opening. "There's someone I think you might want to talk to."

"Who is that?" was the cautious reply.

"Abe Goodman." Hector closed his eyes and tried to picture the man Dean was talking about. Slight, balding, very intense. Wrinkled white dress shirt, shiny blue trousers. Yes, that was Abe. One of those who was only an occasional member of the Crystal group.

"Why Abe?" Hector asked. "What's he want?"

"It isn't what he wants, so much, as what you might need."

"What do I need with a 40-year-old law student?" Hector wanted to know.

"You know he's not a student anymore," Dean replied. "He passed the bar about a year ago, and has just opened his own office."

Why would I need a lawyer, Hector wondered? "Is this to do with that damned committee business?"

"Well, in a way. Look, Hector, couldn't we get together? I really need to explain some things to you, and there are some things you need to know about. We can meet first, and then, if you want, talk to Abe."

"Okay, tell me where and when."

The two men met in a little restaurant on East Capitol Street, about four blocks behind the Library of Congress. It was late in the afternoon, and the tables all around them were empty. The early dinner crowd wouldn't show up for another hour or so.

Hector was already seated when Dean got there. He looked about the room before nodding to Hector and coming to the table. "Having trouble finding me, Dean, or are you worried who might see you with me?" Hector's tone was flat, calm.

"Don't push, Hector," Dean countered. "I'm not ashamed to be seen with you, if that's what you mean." The truce was, at best, uneasy.

"Tell me what this is all about, Dean," Hector said as the larger man sat down opposite him. Hector had sat so that the light was behind him, making Dean's face more easily read.

"Hector, I'm sorry about the way this committee business turned out. I really didn't think it would amount to anything, and that it would just fade away," Dean began. Before he could go on, the waiter came to the table.

"Evenin', Sir. The usual?"

"Yes," Dean nodded.

"And fo' you, Sir?" addressing himself to Hector.

"Just coffee, please."

"Yessir." The waiter moved silently away. Hector looked at the white linen table cloth, smoothed a small crease that stood above the flat surface, and looked at Dean.

"What's 'the usual' Dean?"

"Bourbon and branch," the Southern voice drawled. "Maybe you should relax and have the same."

"I'll stick to coffee. I get the feeling I'll need to be alert here." His smile was only on his lips. "Tell me about Abe, and why I might want to talk to him."

Dean studied this man across from him. "He hasn't talked to me or his sister in weeks, he surely knows that we are more-or-less living together, and he doesn't even ask how she is. Is he a cold man, or do I expect too much," he wondered? At the same time, he began outlining what he thought might be a problem for Hector in the coming weeks.

"You remember how Mr. Folum asked if you had a lawyer, that first day?" Hector nodded his head.

"Well, that was because he thought you might need someone to advise you on what to say."

Congressman Folum, Hector realized, was the man who had first given Dean a job on "The Hill." Perhaps the man was trying to use Dean and his relationship with Hector for his own benefit. Dean had often described him as a politician always running for re-election, and perhaps he thought Hector could provide him with a little extra boost.

"I haven't said anything I didn't mean," he said finally. The waiter came silently to the table and put the drinks down. Noticing that the two men were engaged, he backed away and returned to the dark fringe of the room.

Picking up his drink, Dean took a long swallow.

"You've made a few people angry, you know."

"Your boss, among them?"

"I'm back in the Congressman's office, yes. But no, he isn't angry at all. In fact, I think he kind of admires you."

"What's your position in all of this, Dean?" Hector studied the other man's face as the answer was being prepared.

"Look, Hector, I was offered a temporary assignment on the committee, a chance to be right in the thick of what was going on. I couldn't turn it down. In the first place, it would have killed any chance of getting the job I have now, and making it permanent." The light in his eyes grew more intense as he spoke. "In the second place, it was where things were happening. I needed to be there."

"Did you know what that chairman was going to do, Dean?"

"I did tell you, Hector, that the committee had seen some letters from the 'Warriors at Peace' program, and that they were interested in the organization."

"But you didn't tell me that the chairman was a hard-nosed S.O.B."

"He is that. But he wasn't after you."

"Sounded like it to me."

The two men sat staring at each other for a moment, each waiting for the other to restart the conversation. Finally, Dean resumed.

"I have heard that your publisher is going to drop your contract," Dean said with little emphasis. "You aren't safe, anymore."

Hector just stared at his companion. For perhaps ten seconds he said nothing. Then he looked away, cleared his throat, and said, "Waiter. Bring me one of those." He pointed to Dean's glass.

"And another one for me," Dean said. Now that it was out in the open he felt the need to release a bit more of the tension he had been feeling all day.

Over the next hour, as the bourbon had its effect on the two men, their conversation became less confrontational, and more relaxed. As the restaurant crowd began to drift in, their talk became more careful. It drifted from the possible problem facing Hector's book and livelihood, to Jane, and finally to Sis and Dean.

"Everything still okay with you and Sis?"

"Well, she's worried about you, Hector. And she's been a little cool about this whole hearing business."

"Is that why you decided to call me?"

"No. Yes. But I would have anyway. I just haven't known exactly how you would feel about talking to me, I guess. I'm still your friend, Hector."

"Let's get out of here, Dean. I need to walk."

The office that Abe Goodman could afford was on 14th Street. It was not much bigger than the two-room apartment he had occupied for the last ten years, and not much of an improvement. Short, wiry, his hair cropped close and already marked with gray, Abe was an intense, methodical and driven man. He had returned home from Europe in 1946, and had immediately applied for the GI Bill. He had completed what remained of his undergraduate work in less than two years, and been accepted by the university's law school. But even with his education paid for, Abe still had to work more than he went to school. His father had died before the war, and Abe still supported his mother and younger sister, so it had taken him most of the last ten years to finish law school, about one class a semester. His bar exam behind him, a clerkship in a downtown firm finished, he had opened his solo practice only a month before Dean brought Hector to see him.

"Hello, Hector," Abe had greeted him. "Read your book as soon as it came into the library!" His enthusiastic tone was mitigated by the rather high pitch and eager intensity of his voice. "It's been a while since I've seen you."

"I think the last time was in your apartment when you had your graduation party," Hector recalled.

It had been a small but exuberant party, with most of the core group from The Crystal there to drink beer and eat potato chips. Abe's budget didn't run to much more than that, but it was the kind of party that was more important for its significance than for its amenities. Abe smiled at the recollection. Being a lawyer had been his dream since childhood. Attaining it was and would be the grandest moment in his life.

"Have your own practice now, I see."

"Well, I have this office and I have a few clients, but I'm a long way from having what you would call a 'practice.'" Abe had a wide smile that said everything was just fine.

"Dean thinks I might need your services, Abe," Hector said.

"If what he has told me is accurate, then perhaps I might be of assistance." Hector noted that what had seemed like a pedantic speech pattern was now a professional demeanor. It fit the situation, at least.

"Before we begin," Abe said, "let me ask you a few questions." He had walked behind his desk and seated himself. Drawing a yellow legal pad toward him, and removing a fountain pen from his pocket, he looked up at Hector. "Sit down, both of you." He indicated the pair of chairs facing his desk. As the men settled themselves, Abe went on: "Hector, just so I know where we are, and I remind you that anything we discuss is confidential, does the committee have anything in its files that would implicate you in any manner, in activities against the government?"

Hector looked at Abe, then turned to Dean. "Is there?"

Dean said, in an almost embarrassed way: "I couldn't answer that, Hector."

"Then maybe you shouldn't be here," Hector said softly. There was a silence, and then Dean stood up.

"You're right. Call me later."

"Umm," Hector said. Dean let himself out.

"Does that mean there is?" Hector addressed Abe.

"Not that I know of. But what about you. Answer my question, if you can."

Abe sat back in his chair. With the light from the window behind him, the shadows made him look older, wizened. His white shirt, opened at the collar, looked as if it had been worn more than just one day. There was a sense of old, rather than just age, about him.

"I'm not sure where to begin, Abe. Right after my book was published, I started getting calls from a lot of different people. Some were reporters, some were readers who wanted to say something about the book, about how it had touched them or reflected their own experiences. A few were from organizations of various kinds. One of those was this 'Warriors at Peace.' I had a meeting with their president, a man named Holloway."

Abe nodded. "I know about Mr. Holloway. We've had a few conversations of our own."

"What does that mean?" Hector's interest was immediately energized. "Are you a member?"

Was there some connection, Hector wondered, between Dean and Abe and the committee? Hector rejected the idea of a conspiracy, but was it so far-fetched? In the weeks since the subpoena had arrived, Hector had received a quick education in the theory and practice of conspiracy as perceived by the politicians and the press. He wondered what was really happening here.

"Hector," Abe continued, "I'm not a member. In the first place, I don't join groups, and in the second place, even it I did, I couldn't afford it now anyway. I'm only interested in what you know about what is happening around you."

"What is happening around me?" he wondered to himself. "The people I thought were my friends turn out to be taking advantage of me, and the people who should be protecting what we have are doing their best to destroy it."

Aloud he said, "I don't know, Abe, and I don't understand what is happening around me." It was the best he could offer.

Abe studied his guest, searching for a response that went deeper than "I don't know." There wasn't anything obvious in Hector's behavior, or the way he held himself. He seemed almost too relaxed for a man facing a crisis in his life.

Beginning again, the lawyer outlined what he knew: that Hector had not been helpful or forthcoming before the subcommittee, and so the chairman had reciprocated by not offering a statement that would, in effect, clear the writer from any connection with "un-American activities."

"That is a problem," Abe concluded. Hector waited a moment or two, thinking about what he had been told. Abe said nothing more.

"Why should that be a problem?"

"Because in today's world, Hector, if you aren't 'for 'em, you must be agin' 'em.' In other words, you have made yourself suspect."

"By not telling them something I knew nothing about? I wasn't trying to mislead the committee, Abe. I really don't know anything about the organization, and more than that, I think it's wrong for some bunch of men, appointed or elected, to ask me about my politics and what I believe. In fact, I don't think those are questions any government should be able to ask."

"But they think they have the right to know," the other man said quietly.

Hector looked at Abe, then putting his hands on the arms of the chair, stood and said: "Thanks Abe. I'll have to think about all of this."

"In the meantime," the other said, "you might want to talk to your agent. And if you have any problem with your publisher, come and see me."

It was ten o'clock the next morning when Margery returned Hector's call.

"Damned fools," she said in her well modulated Park Avenue accent, when Hector told her about his conversation with Abe.

"The committee?" Hector asked.

"The committee, too," Margery replied, "but I was thinking about your 'independent' publisher. If it is any consolation, Hector, you are not the only writer being 'reconsidered' right now. You are among a lot of other people in the publishing world, and in Hollywood and a lot of other places who are, as they say, 'under suspicion.'"

"What's happening up there, Margery?"

"Well, in the first place, books and authors are being dropped by publishers at even a hint of a Communist connection. And some of them are damned good writers, and damned fine people. It's not nice here right now."

"Is my book in that group? I'm struggling right now with the new one, and I really need the income to keep me going."

"Keep working, Hector," his agent counseled. "You have some royalties coming in, and the advance might still be available."

With the success of his first book, Hector's publisher had offered a contract and an advance on a second book before the author had even decided to write one. Now he regretted not accepting both.

"Has the publisher said anything?"

"Actually, I spoke with him last week, and he said they were 'reviewing all their authors,' as he put it. I explained to him, in language I am certain he understood, that no self-respecting publisher would even listen to the ranting of those little men in Washington."

Hector smiled. "They aren't little men, Margery."

"By New York standards they are, Hector. They really are."

Chapter 22 - Going Down

When Hector arrived home after his meeting with Abe, he was churning with things to say to Jane, but she was not there. Not unusual, Hector reminded himself. She was working. "Or is she?" The question popped into his mind. It wasn't the first time. He was becoming suspicious of everyone, it seemed. "What is Jane doing?"

Unable to sit patiently, Hector turned and left the apartment. He walked the long city blocks to the Vienna, and as he had on that day more than two years before, when he realized he wanted Jane for more than a friend, he paused at the door, then walked back and forth in front of the restaurant before actually entering.

He looked around. Valery's was the only familiar face. Hector felt his heart skip a beat. Jane was nowhere to be seen! Valery greeted Hector just as though he were still coming in every day for lunch and dinner. As he looked around he answered her questions without thinking, his heart thudding in his chest. Then Jane walked out from the kitchen.

Instantly his face relaxed into a smile. He started toward the side of the room, to his old table, but it was occupied by a middle-aged man, already eating. Hector went to the next table and sat down. Looking up into the dark mirror, his eyes engaged Jane's in the familiar connection.

"Hector," Jane's voice was quiet, caressing her husband's senses, "it has been a long time since you have been in here." Hector looked up, almost smiled, but said nothing. "I'll bring your coffee."

When she returned, Hector asked, "Can you leave early?"

"What's the matter?" Her question was genuine.

"I just don't know what to do."

"I'll talk to Val," Jane said as she walked away.

The diner at Hector's old table stopped eating, looked at Hector appraisingly, and said, "Say, didn't you used to be that famous author? Hector Collin, wasn't that you?"

Hector, turning as if to deflect the impact of "used to be," nodded his head.

"I guess you were some hot stuff till you fell in with the reds, huh?" The man sneered and turned back to his dinner. For a moment Hector stared at him, then abruptly rose from his place, turned and walked out the door, not even pausing where Jane and Valery stood. As the door closed behind him he stopped, shoulders hunched, head forward, unmoving.

"Hector," Jane's voice was tense. "I had to clear it with Val." Her voice was a mix of plaintiveness and affront.

"It wasn't that, Jane. It wasn't you."

"Then what?"

"Just—just everything." His voice was almost a cry.

"Let me get my sweater and we'll go home."

For the first time in their life together, but certainly not in his own, Hector was scared. More than any event in the last few months, the encounter in the restaurant had cut deeply into his none-too-strong shell. He could live with the unfairness of the committee investigation, even with Dean's using him, if he had. And having a contract withdrawn (if that was going to happen), was only a pinprick. But losing the confidence of his readers, of his generation, well that was a blow from which he might not recover. It was a blow from which he might not want to recover.

Hand in hand the couple walked through the lengthening shadows, back across town. The slanting sunlight cast their images behind them. They said nothing more until they reached the apartment. Then, without turning on the lights, they sat close together on the sofa, fingers entwined, his strong arm around her slight shoulders, but he said nothing more.

The windows gave up their sunlight, and the shadows in the room moved upward, now cast by the street lamps.

"Am I a threat to you, Hector?" The question went unanswered.

When had people not been a threat to this man? When in his life had he been in control, he wondered. Had he ever owned his own life? Was this woman a threat? Could he imagine such a thing? Or was it not imagination at all? The thoughts grew and receded eerily in his mind. What was happening to him? Jane's grip on his hands tightened as she felt him starting to pull away.

"Don't go Hector. Don't go away from me, please," she whispered.

Hector didn't go away, but a part of him retreated into a reserve position that slowly closed him off from the threats he felt around him. His daily habits reduced themselves to staying behind the drawn curtains, his desk lamp unlit, his typewriter silent. When the phone rang he ignored it. When there was a knock at the door he closed his ears to the sound. He stared at the blank paper in the typewriter, his mind unfocused, his thoughts diffused.

"I am alone," he wrote one day. "I am on my own to survive or to die." He could write nothing more. His desk, always a model of neatness and order, had become a careless repository of newspapers, unopened mail, and scraps of paper.

The next morning, trying to restore some order to his desk, Jane stared at the line on the page in the typewriter, and turned away.

Days followed one another, phone calls from New York went unanswered, letters remained unopened, conversation between the two stopped.

"Don't go away from me," she had said, yet she was going away from him. Her wonderful Hector was being destroyed in front of her, and she was doing nothing to help him. Her words and her actions implied impatience with his inward-spiraling, devolving self.

She was, in fact, frightened beyond comprehension at the thought of losing this man in whom she had placed her own faith and love; her rock and her protector. She could not face his destruction. "No, no, not Hector," she said to her self. "No, no. Not him." And she wept. The gravity that was driving him inward on himself was at the same time flinging her hard against the surrounding wall. They were as two unlike chemicals in a centrifuge.

The apartment was dark when Jane unlocked the door. That was not unusual. She had often found Hector sitting in the dark these last few weeks. Sometimes it seemed as if he hadn't moved all day. But this was different. The room held the silence of emptiness. Turning on the light, letting her eyes adjust, she looked around. Everything looked the same, yet it was different. It felt different.

In the bedroom Jane found the bureau drawers Hector used emptied of some of his clothes. A shirt or two, a jacket, a suitcase gone from the closet. Turning back to the living room, she went to his desk. All of his papers were there, including some she had never seen before. Copies of his military records, the decorations, and the medals themselves. She picked them up, looked at his name engraved on the backs of them, tried to read the written citations, but she could not see through her tears.

Chapter 23 - Dean Undone

What have you done to my brother?" Sis demanded. She was standing in front of Dean, who had seated himself, as usual, at the small kitchen table. He looked up into the young woman's face, seeing anger and pain he had never imagined. Her voice, usually controlled and modulated as a young lady's should be, was tight with emotion, her lips a thin line, and her eyes afire.

"What?" she repeated.

Dean flinched only a little. For weeks he had been expecting a question like this, expecting it but unable to prevent it. Nor could he answer her. "Why now?" he wondered. "Why has it taken her this long to bring her brother's troubles back to me?" Still he didn't answer.

Calmly, almost whispering, Sis said: "He's gone. Left Jane and gone. Back to New Rhondda." Her voice grew louder as she spoke. "And not a word to anyone. You're responsible for this, Dean, aren't you?"

Without answering, Dean held out his hand, trying to take the one Sis had raised before her. She pulled it out of his reach and stepped back from him.

"I didn't know he had gone, Sis," was all the man could offer. Sis turned abruptly and walked across the room. Hearing Dean stand up, she turned and walked out of the room.

Following slowly behind her, Dean tried to find words to explain, to exculpate himself, to hold on to what he had found, but he realized it was not to be. At last he was able to begin.

"You know I wasn't the instrument of Hector's fall, Sis. That, and all the other bad things, were of Hector's own doing. He was the one who chose to argue with a powerful congressional investigator; he was the one who challenged the man's sincerity; and he, Hector, not me, had been the one to go to the press. Not me, not the committee chairman, but Hector and Hector alone."

Sis's reaction to Dean's outpouring was to continue to walk around the apartment, staying a step or two ahead of the man. Finally, having said all he could, Dean simply stopped, waiting for Sis to do the same. When she realized he was no longer pacing behind her, she did stop, and turned and stood looking up into his face.

"How could you have let him, Dean?"

Dean started over. Again he told Sis how the information had come to the committee, and how he had tried to prepare the way for Hector, but Sis quickly interrupted.

"He's my brother, Dean. Doesn't that count for something in this? Or does Hector simply represent a ticket you need to get 'punched' as you like to put it, on your way up?"

Again Dean stopped. He tried to look into the girl's eyes, but she turned her face away.

From her purse she retrieved a single-page letter. Snapping it open, she waved it at Dean.

"This came from Mama today. Do you have any idea what Hector has done?"

Dean shook his head. "No, Sis. I'd like to know, though."

"He's gone home! He's living in his old room and Daddy is pushing him to join his crew in the mine! In the mine!," she repeated. "He'll bury himself in the damned coal mine! And Jane and I had to find out about it in this little, one page letter from Mama. Oh, Dean. What have you people done to my brother?"

"I told you, Sis. I didn't—we didn't do anything to Hector. He did whatever he did, and now he has gotten himself out of town and hidden away. Maybe that's the best thing he could do right now. Wait 'til all of this blows over and he can come out again."

"Jane," Sis said, "I've sent Dean away."

"Sis, why would you do that?"

"You of all people ought to understand that. He's why Hector is in trouble, and he's why Hector ran away."

"I don't think so, Sis. At least I hope not. I hope what's happened is that Hector just felt he had to get away, not run away. He'll be okay. I know he will. And you and Dean will make up, too." The young women were in the living room of the old apartment.

Sis had asked Jane to come over to talk, and now she said, "Jane, why don't you move back in here? At least for a while? You can't afford the Connecticut Avenue apartment now, and, well, I miss having someone in here."

"I'm not Dean, Sis. Why don't you call him and see if you can work it out? I've got until the end of next month on the lease, anyway, and by then—well, by then everything will probably have worked out, don't you think?"

Sis didn't think, at that point, that anything would ever work out again. Hector was sleeping in their parents' house, being pushed to begin working in the mine, and according to their mother, absolutely uncommunicative.

Hector, his mother had written, was just like his father. A silent breakfast before his father returned at daybreak, then back to his room until supper. Another silent meal, then back to his room, saying not a word to either parent. Every day the same, every night the same. Whatever had happened, the parents neither knew nor understood, nor did their son, in his silence, seem any different from all the other sons of families like theirs. It was simply the way they were. In all of her letters, Mrs. Collin hinted that perhaps it was time for Sis to come home, too.

Chapter 24 - In the Depths, in New Rhondda

For the first several days after his return to New Rhondda, Hector remained in the house, in his room except for meals. He sat on the simple chair, or lay on the narrow bed, his eyes looking, for the first time, beyond his own life. He knew he could not remain hidden in this room, in this house, even in this town for the rest of his days. But what life could he have? What did he want it to be? He had to move on, he knew.

Sitting in the kitchen a week after his arrival, he realized that he had to get out of the house, if even for only an hour. Before leaving the house, he went up to his room and opened his suitcase. The only remnant of his army uniform he had saved, his field jacket, a pair of dark wool pants, and a worn pair of combat boots, were among the clothes he had brought. Changing into the pants, he sucked in his gut to make them fit. The boots were still soft and conformed to his feet. He buckled the canvas tops over his ankles, picked up the old field jacket, and left the house. He walked at his usual pace, neither hurried nor dawdling, as if he had somewhere to go but not soon. The residential streets became more commercial as he descended into the town.

Along Franklin Street, about a block up from the old hotel, was a small shop selling office supplies and books. Hector wanted to write a letter, he thought, to tell Jane what he had done, where he was. On a shelf he found a folder with note paper, envelopes, a place for stamps and a little card explaining postal rates. He took the folder to the counter. There, on a small display rack, was Second Lives. He ignored it, searching his pockets unsuccessfully for the exact change.

"Find what you wanted?" The store owner was a deep voiced woman of perhaps fifty, with tightly curled gray hair and sharp features.

"Yes." Hector, anxious to be on his way, placed money on the counter without looking up. The woman looked at him, and then swiveled her head to look at the book on the counter.

"Hector Collin," she said. It was not accusing, or even surprised, just a statement of fact. Hector picked up the folder and was about to turn and walk out when the woman said, "Don't you want your change?"

Hector was willing to leave the three cents behind, but he turned instead and, taking the coins, said, "Thank you."

"We all liked your book." The conversation wouldn't end. Hector wanted only to leave the store and find his way home. The woman, Grace White, didn't sense the man's discomfort, thinking only that he was in a hurry.

"Come back again," she said as the door closed softly behind him. "Well think of that. I should have asked him to autograph a copy." Grace stared after her customer for a long minute before returning to her business.

At the bottom of the street, Hector remembered, was the small public library, one of the many Carnegie legacies. Turning at the steps leading up to the Greek Revival building, he seemed a little cheered by the prospect of secluding himself behind its quiet walls. In the years since leaving New Rhondda, he had acquired experience, if not knowledge, and acceptance if not understanding, of the larger world. What he had never attempted to work out, however, was how he fit into it all. Now he needed to know.

Except for the librarian, Hector was alone in the room. Miss Martin had been the sole employee of the library as far back as he could remember; a solitary person, happy to be surrounded by books and the soft sounds of the old room. She looked little older. Did she recognize him? He couldn't tell. From time to time he was aware of her appraising gaze, but it could simply be that he appeared as a stranger, rumpled, dressed in old clothes, in need of a haircut, not very prepossessing. Someone to keep an eye on, perhaps, but not a threatening figure.

Hector sat for a long time. The letter folder lay unopened before him. He let his mind take him from this building forward, from his earliest memories of this place. How had he ended up here after so many years away? Was he "home" or was he still moving on? That was what he wanted to think about now, before he could begin to think about what to say to Jane.

As far back as Hector could remember, he had wanted to be somewhere else. In his memory were no significant events or acts that made him feel that way. It was simply that he knew, whether from books and magazines he found in the library, or from stories told by grandparents of places far away, that this town, these mines were not all there was in the world. That was why, he now saw, he had taken the only route open to him when he joined the army so long ago. And his world had opened. He was as at home in Japan as he would have been in Georgia. Hector's world was not wide. It was, however, bigger than he had expected. Meeting and living among people from the larger world had shown him that he was not the only person alone in the world. It allowed him to be himself, and not strive to match an image created by others.

The anonymous life of a soldier had suited him well, he thought. Maybe he should have stayed on, made a career of it. But then, he realized, he would not have met Jane, perhaps not have ever thought of writing a book, yet both had given him true satisfaction and great pleasure. He had liked writing, had loved being with Jane, and felt at home with both of those facets of his life: lover and writer. "Lover." That was a curious term. He loved Jane. And she, he realized, must haved loved him. "Loved?" Could she, after the turns his life had taken, after leaving her without even a scrawled note "goodbye," still love him? What if she didn't. What had he done, he wondered, to that loving girl he had shared the success of his life with? Could she still want him, be with him, be a part of his life?

He considered his writing; how hard it had been. Not finding the words; that had been easy. When the writing was going well the words almost tumbled out too fast. No, it was the transiting between thinking of something he wanted to say, and actually putting the words on paper. He was afraid of that, he understood now. Afraid of committing himself to a piece of paper that would stand over time. He had learned to love the process, had come to feel discontented when he wasn't writing, but in between sessions, almost in between pages, he would sometimes lose the momentum and be unable to restart for hours. It was, he now understood, fear of what others would say when the words were published.

"Isn't it time you had a real job? What else can you do?" Hector considered his father's questions. He wasn't sure if he could do anything else. He felt uncomfortable thinking of himself as a writer, he admitted. Other people made something, or fixed something, or even taught something. What did he, as a writer, really do? His work depended on something others created: a culture, a time, a place. Writing, it seemed to him, was a luxury. Something to do after "work."

Work was, in his mind, something active. Sitting at the typewriter, looking at empty space, or seeing nothing at all, made him feel slightly guilty, as if he were wasting time. Yet the quiet time, minutes or hours, was when his conscious thinking was sublimated, when he examined ideas and feelings, found ways of expressing what was perhaps a revelation even to himself.

Finally Hector reached a point where he could clearly see the two things that mattered most to him: Jane and his writing. He was at last ready to commit himself. Commit to Jane, commit to his next book, and right now, commit his thoughts and feelings to the paper before him, and hope Jane would understand.

In his letter he tried to explain what had happened to him, how desperate he had become in the weeks following the hearing and of being demonized by the press. He wanted her to understand what he now understood: that no matter how much she loved him, in those weeks of struggle he had not recognized her importance to him, the meaning she gave his life.

The letter also tried to place his work in perspective. *I never had a burning ambition to be a writer,* he wrote. *It just sort of came to me, first as part of a class, and then because it seemed easy to do, and because my professor encouraged me. Left to myself, I probably never would even have thought about the people in* Second Lives. *I would simply have gone on until I graduated, and then looked for something else to do.*

Next Hector turned his thoughts to Sis and to Dean. He had been in Washington long enough, he explained to Jane, that he could recognize the pattern his sister's life had taken, and would most likely follow. She was one of so many young women who gravitated to the city; who found themselves part of a community of single men and women. She would, he wrote, be one of those women who never found the satisfaction of a husband and family, but would instead rise in the bureaucracy through devotion to her work and to a boss she might admire, even be in love with. She would have affairs, own a house, take advantage of the cultural life or social life of the sleepy Southern town that was at the same time an international city. Satisfaction would come from her work, but it would be a dry and eventually unsatisfactory life.

From his sister, Hector moved to her first lover and his own erstwhile friend. Dean, he now saw, would forever be grabbing at what he sought, but always just missing it. Dean and his ilk were more committed to politics than to any political ideals. Their lives were built on working for politicians who would help them achieve the power they sought, but Dean was not one who would achieve the status he coveted. He would never be "chief-of-staff" in anyone's office, or direct a congressional investigation on his own. No, Hector felt, Dean was destined to be an assistant, just out of the light shed by the politician he served. And he would always be looking forward apprehensively to the next election, the next change of administration.

When Hector had written all that he had inside him, he had covered nearly a dozen pages. He picked them up and read through them without stopping. He wanted to change nothing. What he had written would have to stand as he had felt it and put in on paper.

Taking a fresh sheet from the folder, he wrote his conclusion: *Of all I have written here Jane, the most important is this: in all my life, my travels, my experiences, the most satisfying, the most rewarding time has been with you. I could go on without you, I'm sure, but I don't know that I really want to. It isn't a matter of you being there for me, but of our being there for each other. I knew I wanted you, I knew I needed you, and I think you felt the same way. I truly believe that with you beside me I will find a way to be the writer I started out to be; find a way to make my voice heard. I will continue to say the things I believe need to be said, in a way that might make a difference. Deep in my soul I believe that the times we are going through, personally and politically, will eventually be reversed and good sense will prevail. I am just as certain that these times will likely come again, and that voices like mine will still be heard, once the clamor and confusion die away. I want to be there when it does. And I want you with me all the way. One last thought, Jane. You and Sis and some others have called me a hero. If I was a hero, it was an accident. It was not something I set out to be. But really, all heros are accidental, aren't they?*

He signed the letter, assembled the pages, folded them and put them into an envelope. Looking up, he realized that the light from the windows had changed, that it was now afternoon, and the day was working to its close. He addressed the envelope, put away his pen, now nearly out of ink, and stood up. He was a little stiff from the long hours he had sat bent over the letter, and his first steps were a little tentative, almost as if he were learning to walk again as he had after he was wounded in Korea. Smiling at Miss Martin, he walked to the front door and went out.

It had been snowing. The ground and the roofs had a frosting of white, a clean, crisp smell in the air. A new world for a new beginning. Hector's footprints were the first in the new, white snow.

THE END